IT'S TIME MY DARLING

Written By: Amber Dayne

Writers Guild Registration: R06680-00

Date Registered: December 28, 2001

Order this book online at www.trafford.com
or email orders@trafford.com

Most Trafford titles are also available at major online book retailers.

Printed in Victoria, BC, Canada.

ISBN: 978-1-4269-2191-9 (soft)
ISBN: 978-1-4269-2556-6 (hard)

Library of Congress Control Number: 2010900113

*Our mission is to efficiently provide the world's finest, most comprehensive book publishing
service, enabling every author to experience success. To find out how to publish your
book, your way, and have it available worldwide, visit us online at www.trafford.com*

Trafford rev. 2/2/2010

 www.trafford.com

North America & international
toll-free: 1 888 232 4444 (USA & Canada)
phone: 250 383 6864 ♦ fax: 812 355 4082

Summer of 1997

Alice parks her car in her spot and reaches for the package on the back seat. She looks into the mirror to make sure her hat is on right and opens the door and casually climbs out.

"Good morning, Alice," Joe the guard smiles cheerfully at her.

"Good morning, Joe. Lovely day isn't it?" Alice smiled.

"Sure is." As he opens the door for her.

"Thank you." Alice smiles. "Anything interesting happen today?" Should I be on my awares while I'm in here?"

"No ma'am. Everything has been quiet."

"So far huh?" Alice laughs.

"Yeah so far." Joe nods to her.

Alice walks up to the desk. "Good morning, Mary." Holding up the package. "I have something for Janie. May I go in?"

Mary shakes her head. "I don't know about you. Your day off. Don't you have anything better to do?"

"You know how important things are to her, Mary. Besides it's her birthday."

"Go on in." Shaking her head as she buzzes the door.

Alice knew right where she'd find Janie too. Sitting in the window and watching the birds. She paused and watched as Janie excitedly exclaimed, "look. Look there's one flying." She put her hands together and smiled brightly. Alice walks over to her.

Janie crouches away from her as she reaches out to her. "Here sweetie." Holding out the package. "I have something for you."

Janie's eyes meet Alice's as she slowly reaches out.

"Go on. It's for you." Alice smiles very warmly at her.

"Janie's head jerks back to the window. "Look a bird flying." She takes the bag. "For me?" She asks hesitantly.

"Yes, dear it's for you." Alice smiles very warmly at her.

Janie sits down and carefully opens the package and pulls out a book. On the cover is a beautiful picture of birds and other animals and flowers. Her face lights up. "Oh look. Birds and things."

"Open it, dear." Alice urges her. "There's lots more inside." Alice sits down beside her. As they turn the pages together she doesn't notice that she is being watched by a man across the room. She is laughing with Janie as she watches her expressions and joy of the pictures as she turns the pages. Finally they reach the end and Alice stands up.

"Now remember, Sweetie. This is your book." She pushes it into Janie's arms. "Okay?" Smiling as Janie shakes her head vigorously. As Alice turns to leave the man across the room casually strolls ahead of her. She stops at the door and looks back to see Janie looking through the book again. Smiling, she starts down the hall. She notices a man trying a door that is for employees only. She hurries over to him as he opens the door and steps inside.

"You can't go in there. Hey, somebody. That door is supposed to be locked." As she opened it and stepped inside, she is grabbed, and the door is pulled shut. A hand covers her mouth as she is dragged to the back of the linen closed. She struggles but it does her no good. Slowly her struggles cease and she slumps to the floor. The man quickly takes his clothes off and undresses her, and puts hers on. He puts her body at the back of the closet and covers her with some linens and towels. As he straightens the dress he notices the flatness of his chest. He looks around, gets two wash cloths, and puts them in a bra. He then took her wig and hat and put them on. Picking up her purse and taking a deep breath, he opens the door and walks out.

At the entrance, Mary looks up, and seeing Alice, buzzed the door to let her past. Alice waved as she walked through the door and out to freedom.

****

3

I

Jessie pulls the car into the garage. She sits there for a few seconds and then gets out still singing the song that had been playing on the radio. She goes into the house and peers into the living room to let her mom know she was home.

"Hi, mom."

"Hi, sweetie," as she looks at her daughter. "How was the shower?"

"It was great. Lorie got a lot of cute baby clothes. She was so thrilled that everybody came that she cried."

Her mother smiled knowingly. "I know exactly how she felt." She sighed. "When I was pregnant with you and the shower was a success. I got a little emotional myself."

"Why does that happen?" Jessie asked curiously.

"I suppose it's because at that stage you're already emotional," she sighs, "about the way you look and everything seems to affect you. That's just the way it is."

"Well, she made a lot of us teary eyed too." Jessie smiled remembering.

Her mom smiled at that. "If you didn't have a reaction, Jessie, I would think there was something wrong with you."

"So it is a natural thing then? I was beginning to think of us as a bunch of softies."

Her mom laughs at that. "I'd much rather see you a softie than a person who is affected by little or nothing at all."

"I know a person like that." She makes a face. "Thank God I'm not like her."

Her mother stands and offers her the control. "Do you want this?"

"No. I think I'll get some juice and read the comics. I never had a chance to do that today."

"I think I'll get ready for bed. I had a hard time going back to sleep this morning."

"Night, mother. Love you."

"Love you too sweetie. Night."

Jessie goes into the kitchen and pours herself a glass of juice, and sitting down at the table, picks up the comics. She looks for Hagar first. That was her favorite and then Garfield. She smiled at that. Garfield. I couldn't imagine having a cat like that. I'd strangle him for sure.

Smiling at that thought as she read his caper for today. She finished her juice and decided to sit on the porch for a while hoping that Jake would call her. It had been a couple of days since she had heard from him and he never went more than that before picking up the phone and calling her. She gets the phone and sits on the swing. It was such a beautiful night that she wished he was here with her. It would be nice to sit in his arms. The thought made her smile. She knew that she had fallen in love with him. When she wasn't sure, but she definitely loved him. She pictured him in her mind. Tall and dark, and oh so handsome.

She knew that there was a few girls who drooled over him, but he seemed only to notice her. At least she hoped it was that way. She did notice a few nasty looks coming her way on different occasions and there was this one girl in particular that got downright nasty about it sometimes. This girl who professed to be a friend, tried with all her body to entice Jake. It didn't work. She sighed. Not that she knew of anyhow. She looks up at the stars and yawns. Maybe she should wish upon a star. The phone rings and she picks it up.

"Hello," she says distantly.

"Hi," Shelly said. "What are you doing? You sound as if you were in another world."

"I'm sorry, Shelly. I didn't mean to. I was just sitting, looking at the stars, thinking about you know who."

"Ah," Shelly said meaningfully. "Jake again huh?"

"Yes, I'm afraid so." She sighed. "Did you need something?"

"No. It's just to nice to go to bed so I thought I'd chat with you for a bit."

"Wasn't Lorie's shower nice? You know, it was all I could do to keep from crying when she did."

"I hear you. I think just about everyone there had tears except for Lynn. But then that's nothing new. I swear if I was like her, Jessie, I would lock myself away."

7

Jessie laughs at that. "Thank God You're not. Who could stand two of her around?"

"Have you ever wondered how she became a part of our group? I mean, she is totally different from every one of us. Jenny, Pam, Lorie and Lena. We all have similar personalities and then there is Lynn. Way out in left field."

"That's a good way to put it," Jessie laughs. "We should feel bad about the way we cut on her, but you know what. I don't. Not in the least."

"I know for a fact that you're not the only one that feels like that." Shelly sighs. "Enough about her. Let's think about something pleasant."

"And I know exactly what that would be," Jessie laughs.

"Let me have two guesses." Shelly laughs. "Jake and Jake."

Jessie laughs with her. "And you'd be right both times. Actually I was dragging my feet about going to bed hoping he'd call me."

"look, one of mothers friends is trying to beep in. I'll talk to you later."

"Bye." Sighing Jessie decides she should go to bed. Putting the phone back, and locking the door, she slowly climbs the stairs. Half way up she hesitates and comes back down to see what's on TV. She finds a movie called Mercury Rising with Bruce Willis and decides to watch it. Getting a pop and the chips she plops into her favorite easy chair and melts into it. She had just popped a chip into her mouth when the phone rings.

"Hello," she said muffled.

"Are you munching?" Shelly asked her.

"Uh-huh. On chips. I'm watching a movie too."

"It's a wonder you don't look like a chip." Shelly laughs at her.

Jessie Laughs too. "I know, but what can I say. I just have a weakness when it comes to them."

"What are you watching?"

"It's called Mercury Rising with Bruce Willis. It looks like it is going to be pretty good. You know me. I like mystery and murder movies and that's what this is."

"Well, I'll let you go so you can watch it in peace. I'll call you tomorrow."

"Okay." She puts the phone down and settles back to watch the movie. When it was over she stands and stretches. Putting the chips away she goes up to get ready for bed. Sitting on the edge of her bed, she reaches for a picture of Jake and touches it gently. He is so handsome. Putting it back and lying down she smiles. They'd had a pretty good summer so far. He'd been attentive and spent a lot of time with her, but had yet to ask her to be his girl. What she'd love was to be his wife. This thought made her smile. She was sure he loved her, but he never said as much. Mrs. Jessica Lansing. Now that had a wonderful sound to it. And what a wife she intended to be. She would do whatever it took to make him happy. And she knew that she'd have no trouble what so ever loving him for the rest of her life. Mrs. Lansing. She loved the sound of that. Mrs. Lansing, you have a call on line two. Mrs. Lansing, you have a package. She smiled at her childish thoughts. But then I guess love does that to you no matter how old you are. She smiles as her eyes droop. Yes I can see myself very well as Mrs. Lansing.

Amber Dayne

She's running. She's panting for her breath. Glancing over her shoulder as she hears heavy breathing and footsteps, but all she sees is mist. She searches frantically, still trying to find what it is she's running from. She stumbles and tries desperately to keep from falling. She looks back and sees coming from the mist a man. He's wearing a pink polka dot dress and a blonde wig. His arms reach out for her and she tries to run faster. There's the house. She knows she must reach the house. Glancing back again she sees him reaching for her top. She runs onto the porch just as he grabs her top and tries to pull her back. She screams and it wakes her up.

She sits up grabbing her chest, rocks back and forth. Sweat running down her brow. She is trembling all over.

Her mother comes into the room. "What is it Jessica? Not another dream?" She sits on the bed.

Jessie falls into her arms. "Oh mother. This time he touched me! He grabbed my shirt."

Sighing her mother said "I wish I knew what to do Sweetie. But I really haven't a clue. If he is getting close enough to touch you, maybe we need should try to find out what they mean.

Jessica looked at her, "if we could just figure out why I started having them." She pushes the hair back from her face. "Let's just wait and see what happens. Maybe they'll stop as fast as they started."

"If they don't we can always seek help." Her mother suggested.

Jessie starts laughing.

"What's so funny?" Raising her brow in puzzlement?

"You should of seen him. He had on this pink polka dotted dress and blonde wig. He looked simply awful." She shuddered. "I saw him real good this time. Snarling as he reached for me."

Standing her mother said softly, "try to go back to sleep. It's still to early to get up."

Jessie they there thinking about the dreams she's been having lately. What could they mean? Actually why had they started in the first place?

She knew that dreams usually have a meaning. Especially something of this sort. Something must have triggered them. But what? What had she done that would bring such dreams on?

Maybe it wasn't her at all, but someone else had caused them to start. She felt thirsty so she goes to the kitchen to get a drink. She sits at the table and stares out the window wishing she'd dream of something instead of these God awful dreams she'd been having. Like Jake. Smiling at that.

She decides to go to the library and see if she can find something on dreams or maybe intuitions that might give her an idea of what she was dealing with. If it had deeper meanings than she could understand then she'd have to take her mothers advice and talk to someone who could help.

Could this mean that she is somehow troubled and something about it is finally coming out? She shuddered at that thought. It can't be that. She was sane. She had no deep dark secrets. Her childhood had been wonderful. Her parents were both very supportive and loving. She had wanted for nothing so what could they mean?!

She decided to go back to bed and promised herself to go to the library first thing. Maybe, just maybe she'd be able to figure this all out and be done with it.

She lay staring at the ceiling. Each time she dreamed it was getting clearer and what started as a misty fog no had some sort of sound and a person showing himself. And what a strange person he seemed to be. A dress and a wig What could that mean? That usually is associated with a cross dresser or someone who has had a sex change. But she didn't know anyone like that. What if were a sign of something to come. That this could be intuition maybe? But she'd never had anything like this happen before. Dreams like this just don't start for no apparent reason do they? She felt both chills and excitement as to maybe she was on to something. She rolls onto her side. Maybe I'll talk to Shelly and we can do this together. Or maybe Jake. Ah, yes, Jake. That's what she needed to think about. Her eyes droop.

She is awakened by a loud bang. She sits straight in her bed and looks around. She stretches and gets up and dresses and goes down to the kitchen.

"Morning, mother." She smiles.

"I didn't mean to wake you." Carol apologized. "I dropped a pan."

"That's alright. I needed to get up." Pouring a glass of juice. "Are we going shopping today? We haven't done anything together for a while and I'd like to shop." Smiling mischievously. "What better way to spend time than shopping.

Her mother smiled at her. "Shopping huh?"

"Yea. I saw this dress I want to get for Lena's wedding."

"I hope you're going to try it on first." Carol advised.

"Of course I am, but don't you think I can wear just about anything, mother. "After all I take after you."

Laughing at her Carol sets her breakfast before her. "Thank you, but I don't look good in everything." She emphasized.

"Sure you do." Jessie replied as she took a bite. "All my friends say that about you. That you can wear anything and look good."

"Well, thank your friends for me." Carol rinses her cup. "I'll get dressed while you finish eating."

Jessie had just finished her juice when she heard a knock on the door. She got up to answer and froze in her tracks. There standing outside the door was the man in her dreams. The one that had chased her. Wiping her hands on her shorts and swallowing she steps to the door.

"Is Carol here?" He smiled at her.

Trying not to sound callous she asks, "May I ask what you want?"

He sensed some sort of vibes here, but answered, "I'm here at her request. I sell insurance and she wants to get some extra coverage." He pauses. "If this a bad time I can come back."

Turning to the stairs she hollered, "Mother, can you come down here? There is a gentleman to see you."

"Be right down." As she comes to the top of the stairs.

"How rude of me," Jessie opens the door, "please come in."

"You must be Jessica?" Smiling as he offered his hand. "I'm Dave."

She takes his hand. "Yes, I'm Jessica. Actually everybody calls me Jessie." She pulled her hand away and turns as her mother came to the bottom of the steps. Smiling she shakes her hand in front of herself and pursing her lips, waves her brows signaling he's hot.

Her just mother just smiled as she steps up to Dave.

Jessie wipes her hands on her shorts and goes back to the kitchen to rinse her plate and glass. She's so bothered by this man that she forgets to turn on the cold water and drops the plate.

Her mother came into the kitchen. "What happened? Are you alright?

"I'm sorry. I wasn't paying attention to what I was doing and burnt my hands." Jessie gave a wane smile. "Sorry."

"Be more careful," her mother whispered.

Jessie picks up the phone, but pauses before she dials as she hears her mother laugh. She sighs and dials the number.

"Shelly? Hey, what are you doing today?"

"Probably nothing. Why? What's up?"

"Do you want to go shopping with me and my mom?"

"Beats sitting around the house all day. When will you be over?"

"Probably at least an hour or so. There's this insurance person here and you know how those things go." Jessie laughed.

"Yea, I know. I'll be ready whenever you get here."

"Okay. Bye." Jessie replaces the phone and pauses as she hears her mother laughing. Turning to go upstairs she hears her mother call to her. She peeked into the living room. "Did you want me?"

"Yes I did. Would you mind going shopping without me? Dave asked me to ride upstate with him," smiling hopefully, "and I thought it would be a nice change."

"Not at all, mother." She smiled sweetly even though she was churning inside. "I called Shelly and she's going too. So go ahead and enjoy yourself and don't worry about me." Waving her brows. "Besides, I'll have fun spending your money."

They all laugh and Dave stands and offers his hand again. "It was nice meeting you, Jessie."

"It was nice meeting you too." She pulled her hand away and raced up the stairs. She grabs her purse and keys and runs back down the stairs and at the bottom bumps into Dave. He put out his hands to steady her. "Thanks. I should watch where I'm going." Kissing her mom's cheek, "have a good time today."

As she pulls away she sees Dave open the car door for her mother. Besides being good looking he's also a gentleman she thought. But he was also the man in her dreams and she wasn't so sure she her mother should be going off with him like that.

Jessie taps on Shelly's door and walks in.

"Hey, I thought you said an hour or so?" She exclaimed.

"Oh, that sales person wanted mother to go somewhere with him. So she's sending alone. Got lots of money?"

"What's lots?" Shelly hedged.

"Enough to go to J C Penny's? They're having a sale and we could get some good buys for school."

"School," Shelly wrinkled her nose, "what a dirty word."

Jessie laughs. "Dirty word or not, It's something that we have to do."

"Miss Practical here." Shelly scoffed.

"Miss Practical is going to be rich one day and school is the start." Jessie looks at Shelly and sees her shaking her head. "What?" Spreading her hands.

"What are we going to do with you?"

"You are going to love me just the way I am." Jessie replied smugly.

"You're probably right. Again." Shelly added.

Just smiling Jessie asks, "Ready?"

They made quite a morning of it. The dress she wanted was perfect so she purchased it. They did a lot of window shopping and found several good buys for their wardrobe.

"Is it lunch yet? I'm hungry." Shelly complained.

"Past lunch time," Jessie laughed as her stomach growled. See what I mean?"

After a quick lunch they went back to Shelly's house and Jessie helped carry her stuff in. "It looks like we bought out the store."

Laughing Shelly agreed. "It does doesn't it?"

Plopping down on the bed Jessie asked, "have you heard from Dan?"

"No I haven't. Not for a couple of days."

"I haven't heard from Jake either. I wonder why?"

"I haven't a clue, but if I don't hear from him by tomorrow, I'm calling him." Shelly stated.

"Yea, me too. I'm not about to let that one get away." Jessie exclaimed.

"The way he is with you?" Shelly frowned at her. "I don't see that happening!"

"I hope you're right." Jessie sighed deeply. "I've fallen for him you know?"

"I thought as much. And to be perfectly honest I think he's been in love with you for some time now." Shelly stated.

"Do you really think so?" She walks to the window. "I keep hoping that he will do or say something, anything to let me know how he feels."

"You know what guys are like, Jessie. They do things in their own good time and their own way." Shelly smiled sadly. "I learned that from my dad."

"Men! Or should I say boys?" Jessie laughed at that. "Because most of them act that way don't they?"

"Yes, but what would we do without them?" Shelly chided.

"Let's not think about that. I'd rather think about being held in his arms, of being kissed." Jessie dreamed out loud.

"Stop it," Shelly laughed out. "You're making me want to call Dan right now."

"Now there's an idea." Jessie said quickly.

"Oh no!" Shaking her head. "I'm not doing it."

"Chicken." Jessie teased.

"You do it then." Shelly challenged back.

Jessie shakes her head. "No. We'll wait on them."

"Now who's the chicken?" Shelly challenges her.

"Oh alright. I'll do it." She gets the phone and dials.

"May I speak to Jake please?" She ask sweetly.

"He's out in the shop working. Can I take a message?" Susan asks her.

"Would you tell him Jessie called. He hasn't called for a couple of days and I wanted to see if he's okay."

"Yes, I'll do that." As an after thought, "they've been really busy the past couple of days. They haven't had much time for anything else."

"Okay. Thank you. Bye." Jessie says to Shelly as she hangs up, "his mom says they have been really busy."

"So that's why?" Shelly breathed a sigh. "I knew there had to be a reason."

"Whew!" Jessie breathed out. "But I still wish they had called."

"Just like we said, they don't think of things like that. We're taken for granted." Shelly stated matter of factly.

"Maybe we shouldn't be around when they do call." Jessie sulked.

"But I don't want to make Dan mad!" Shelly exclaimed.

Laughing Jessie says, "I can see he's going to wrap you around his little finger."

"No he won't." Shelly responds stubbornly.

"Yes he will and there's nothing wrong with that. Except sometimes you have to act like you're in control.

"And I think you're in for a stormy relationship if you keep thinking that way!" Shelly shot back.

Jessie throws back her head and laughs. "You wouldn't be getting a little angry would you, Shelly?" She hugs her. "I must be going home. I have the breakfast dishes to do and put all my stuff away too." As she walks to the door. "You're not angry at me are you?"

"No," Shelly laughs. "Maybe just a bit miffed."

Jess pulls her car into the garage and gathers her packages and carries them to her room. Laying aside the dress she wanted to show her mother. She hears a car door and looks out to see Dave come around and open the door for her mother. He offers his hand and smiling she takes it. They stand there and talk for a few moments then she pulls her hand away and walks to the house. He watches her and Jessie watches him. He looks up and she stands perfectly still as he gets into his car.

A light tap on her door. "How'd your day go?" Looking at all the packages. "Very well I see." Carol teases her.

"Yes, we had a good time." Reaching for the dress. "This is the one I was telling you about." Holding it in front of herself.

Carol touched it gently. "Powder blue. My favorite color." She looks at Jessie with smiling eyes. "I bet you look beautiful in it."

"It does look really nice on. Shelly got it in a soft green and it is pretty too." Turning to her mother. "So how was your day?"

"I had a very nice time." She sighed as she smiled. "He is very good company. Always polite, witty just plain good company." Carol sits on the bed. "What's bothering you, Jessie?"

"Where did you meet him?" Jessie didn't answer.

"At the office. One of the girls has insurance with him." She sighs again. "He's really a nice sort, Jessica."

"I'm sure he is. Just be careful, okay." Jessie looks away. "I lost a father, I don't want to lose a mother too."

"Why on earth would say a thing like that, Jessica!?" Carol asks exasperated.

"I don't really know, mother. Just promise me you'll be careful." Jessie pleads.

"Alright, sweetie, for whatever reason, I promise." Carol stands. "But I want you to be nice to him."

"Are you going to start seeing him?" Jessie countered.

"Would you mind?" Carol questioned back.

"No, I don't suppose I would." Jessie closes the closet door. "I'm going down to do the dishes and then and then I think I'll get ready for bed. I'm tired tonight."

"It has been a long day." Carol stands. "I'm going to turn in too. Night, Jessie."

"Night, mother. Love you." Jessie says as she walks down stairs.

"Love you too, sweetie."

As she lay in her bed later, she tries to visualize every part of the mans face that spent the day with her mom. She is certain he is the one chasing her in her dreams. The man in the pink polka dot dress and blonde wig. Her eyes droop and she jerks awake and rolls onto her side. She stares at the clock as her eyes droop again and she sleeps.

She's running. The thick mist is everywhere. Glancing back sees nothing, but she feels this intense fear. She must reach the house. But her feet are so heavy. She tries to cry out, but nothing comes from her mouth. Looking back again she sees a form coming out of the mist. It's not the same one. It's the upper part of a body. It's skin is bluish-grey and it has these large black eyes with fluorescent rings around them. He's floating not walking towards her, reaching out to her as he gets closer. She looks frantically for the house . Just as she sees it the other one emerges from the mist. Arms outstretched to her. As he touches her she screams.

She sits up and swings her legs over the side of the bed. She's panting for her breath when her mother comes rushing in. Carol sits down and holds her 'til her breathing slows down.

"Bad this time huh, sweetie?" Carol asks softly.

Jessie pushes her hair back. "This time there was two of them. As if it isn't bad enough facing one of them, now there's two!"

"They're the same?" Carol puzzled.

"No. No I should have stated that differently." She sighs. "The other one was like a half a person. It was floating and had these huge black pupils with green fluorescent rings. It's skin is grayish." She shuddered. "Those eyes stared right through me. Evil.." Her voice faded.

"Something must have triggered this, sweetie. Something that was said maybe." Sighing deeply. "I just don't know." They sat in silence for a few seconds. Carol stands and touches Jessie's face. "I'm going back to bed. It's way to early to get up and I have to be at the office today. You should try to get some sleep too."

"I'm going down to have some hot chocolate. I don't want to sleep yet." Jessie stands.

"Alright." Carol understands. "Night again.

Reaching for her mothers hand. "I'm sorry I keep waking you up with these stupid dreams." Jessie apologizes.

"That's alright, Jessica. What are mothers for?" Carol smiles gently.

"I don't think it's to be woke up by your teenage daughter." Jessie laughed.

She goes down to the kitchen and fixing her drink carries it to the living room. She sits in the darkness and sips. She didn't want to think about her dream, but she couldn't help it. What was the second one? A person or a thing? It looked dead with it's grayish skin and those eyes. Those evil looking eyes! She shuddered. It had to be a person. But who? She set her cup down and laying her head back closed her eyes.

She hears water running and opening her slowly realizes it's coming from the kitchen. She stands and stretching let's out a low groan. Picking up her cup she goes to the kitchen.

"What are you doing up?" Raising a brow at her. "Or didn't you go back to bed?"

"No," as she yawned. "I fell asleep in the chair." She pours a glass of juice.

"Do you want to eat breakfast with me?" Holding out eggs.

"No thanks. I'm not hungry." Yawning again. "I guess I wasn't ready to get up yet."

"What are you doing today?" Carol asked as she buttered her toast."

"Probably nothing. Unless Shelly wants to do something. If I do decide to do anything I'll call you." She kisses her mom's cheek. "I can't have you worrying about me."

"I don't worry about you." Carol said frankly.

"Joke, mother." She laughs.

"Well, don't get into any trouble." Carol joked back.

"As if, mother." Jessie went to her laughing. She makes her bed and sits down and is deep in thought when her mother calls to her. She goes to the top of the stairs.

"I'm leaving now. You be sure and call me." Carol orders.

"I will, mother. Have a good day." She dresses and goes down to her moms breakfast dishes. As she puts the last glass away the phone rings. She smiled as she looked at the caller ID. "Hello." She said sweetly."

"Hi, Jessie. What are you doing?" Jake asked.

"I'm cleaning house." Softly.

"Do you want to do something today?" He sighs.

"What did you have in mind?" Smiling from ear to ear.

"I thought we could go to the beach. Hang around for most of the day, then get a bite to eat and take in a movie." He paused. "I mean if that's alright with you?" He cleared his throat. "So just say the word and we're on."

"Yeah, I'm up for that. What's Dan and Shelly doing?" Jessie asks.

"I'm picking Shelly up. Dan's already here." He paused again. "I called you back last night."

"Oh did you?" Jessie said disappointingly. "I went to bed early. I was really tired."

"So we're on then?" Jake questioned.

"Oh yeah," Jessie laughs. What she felt like saying was; are you out of your mind? Of course we're on.

"Okay then." Jake laughs at her response. "I'll be there in a bit."

"Bye." Jessie hangs up and does a dance around the table. She suddenly felt lighter. She finishes the dishes and is dancing around the living room when the phone rings. "Hello." Jessie breathes.

"What are you doing? You sound all out of breath." Shelly asks.

"Oh, I was just dancing around a little bit. What's up?"

"Are you going today?" Shelly laughs knowing this was a dumb question.

"Are you nuts!? Of course I'm going!" They both laugh.

"Are you wearing your new bathing suit?" Shelly chuckles, knowing the answer again.

"Oooh yesss." Jessie drawled. "And you?"

"You bet. I've got to look my best today." Shelly giggles. "Isn't this great? The two most gorgeous guys in town and we're spending the day with them!"

"Amen," Jessie echoed. "Look. "I'm going to get off here and call my mom. I told her that if we decided to do anything I'd call her."

"Okay. I'll see you after bit." She pulls the away, but hears Jessie say something.

"Shelly?" Jessie hesitated.

"Yeah, what is it?" Shelly sensed something wrong.

"Why don't you plan on spending the night? I need to talk to someone I can trust." Jessie whispered.

"What's wrong, Jessie?" Shelly asks concerned.

"We'll talk later. It's nothing to worry over, I just need to talk about something. Personal." Jessie added.

"Alright. I'll spend the night." Shelly promised.

"Okay. I'll see you in a bit then. Bye." Jessie dials her mom's office. "May I speak to Carol please?" She walks to the window and looks out. "Hi, mom. I said I'd call you. Jake called and wants to spend the day at the beach."

"That's nice, sweetie. Have a good time, but be careful."

"I will. Shelly's spending the night. Okay?" Jessie added.

"Sure it's okay." Carol laughs.

"So we'll probably eat out too." As an after thought.

"Well then I wont fix supper. Unless you all want to come to the house to eat?" Carol offered.

"I doubt it. And if I'm late I love you and I'll see you in the morning." Jessie said lovingly.

"I love you too. Bye, sweetie." Carol says softly.

"Bye, mother." Jessie hangs up and then dials another number. "Jake? Hey what time was you planning on picking me up?"

"Around eleven or so. What's up?" Jake asked.

"Nothing really. I was wondering if I had time to run to the library?" Glancing at the clock. "It's nine now so I should time. I didn't want to leave and miss you." Jessie said hurriedly.

"I'll call before I leave. That way I can wait if your not back yet." Jake offered.

"I shouldn't be gone all that long, but yes, call."

"See you after bit then." Jake replied.

Jessie grabs her keys and heads for the library. Once there she looks through several books on dreams and visions, but finds nothing that would be of any help. Then she spots one on Intuition and ESP. Looking through them she knew that she found what she needed. Now maybe she would get to the bottom of this.

Back at the house she takes the books to her room and laid them on her bed. She stared at them for a second and went to pick one up, but lay it right back down. She put on her bathing suit and put together her beach bag and went down stairs to the kitchen and got a drink. She was sitting and staring out the window when the phone rang and she jumped."Hello," Jessie said softly.

"What?! Oh don't say that." She cried.

Jake laughed. "Got ya. Just joking, Jessie." Jake's still laughing when he says, "be there in a few minutes."

Just you wait. She thinks as she hangs up the phone. She's sitting on the porch watching a bird when she hears a horn beeping.

"Very funny." Jessie gives him a look. "Hi, guys. I'm ready for a simply splendid day." Spreading her arms.

They laugh at her as she bounces into the car. "Why are you in such a good mood?" Jake teases.

Jessie pouts. "My feelings are hurt now."

"I'm just teasing." Jake squeezes her hand.

"Besides I'm always in a good mood. Aren't I Shelly?"

"Yep, you are." Shelly pushed Jakes shoulder. "You'd better watch it, buster. There's two of us to your one."

"Yea? What about Dan?" Jake smarted back at her.

"Ha ha," Shelly mocks a laugh, "not if he knows what's good for him."

Dan just smiled sheepishly.

"Aw, come on." Jake smarted off to him. "We guys have to stick together."

Clearing his throat Dan said, "I don't think this is one of those times."

"Give me a break, man!" Jake exclaims.

Jessie tickles him under the chin. "What's the matter, sweetie?"

Jake didn't answer.

"Cat got your tongue?" Jessie asks sweetly.

Shelly reaches up and tweaks his ear. "Poor Jake."

He pushes her hand away. "Okay. So It' you two against me. I can handle that."

"We'll see about that," Jessie teases mischievously.

As he pulls into the parking lot at the beach Jake gives her a look of his own. Eyes dancing his expression told her to be alert.

She smiled back, Jessie loved a challenge. "Look how inviting the water is today." Jessie sighed. "Are we ready?" And they run down the beach and straight into the waves.

They were all tanning later when Jake asks, "So what is everybody hungry for? Fast food or restaurant?"

"Burger king." Jessie said simply.

"Yea," the others agreed, "that sounds good.

Jessie jumps up. "Let's go then 'cause I'm hungry."

"Me too," Shelly jumps up and stretches. "I think I'll have two whoppers, fries and a large drink. Oh yea, and a pie."

Jessie looks at her in mock horror. "Shelly! You eat like that and it won't be long until you're a size sixteen!"

"Just joking, guys." She wiggles her body moving her hands down her shape. "I like me just the way I am."

Dan waves his brows. "Me too."

Everybody laughs. Waving at their friends as they pile into the car.

Jake grabs Jessie's hand. "Are we going to a movie afterwards?"

"Let's go to my house." Shelly offered. "We can set on the deck and if we want play in the pool."

Jake looks at Dan. "Any complaints with that?"

"Fine by me," Dan answered.

"Me too," Jessie agreed.

"Good. Now let's eat." Shelly ordered.

"Getting bossy, aren't we?" Jake smarted at her.

"Hunger makes you do thing s like that." Shelly smarted right back. "Besides, somebody has to get your butt moving!"

"You little bitch!" As he lunges for her.

Shelly squeals and ducks behind Dan, who's laughing at her.

After Burger King they go to Shelly's and she says into the living room, "hi, mom. We're going out onto the deck and hang."

"Hi, kids," She smiles and waves at them.

Shelly looked at Jessie. "What did you want to talk to me about?" She whispered.

"Maybe we should wait until we're alone." She whispered back.

"I see," Jake pouted, "we're not good enough to hear anything."

"No, silly." Jessie laughs. "It's not that." Looking at him for a long moment. "Do you promise not to make fun, either of you?!" Looking at Dan too.

"Scouts honor." They said together.

"I'm serious, guys." Jessie chided.

"So are we," Jake said seriously.

"You know you can't trust me," Shelly whispered.

Jessie sits down. Clearing her throat. "I don't know exactly how to start this." Looking at Shelly. "Do you believe in intuitions?"

"I do." Dan spoke up.

Jessie looked at him. Warmed by the sincere look on his face.

"Yes, I do." Shelly answered her.

"Well," she pauses, "about a month ago, I started having these dreams. Bad dreams. At first I'm just running. I don't know why. I'm just doing it. I have this fear that something is after me. I'm gripped in this terrible mist, and whatever it is, I'm afraid of is in there too. The mist is everywhere. I can't see a thing. Then about a week ago, a man came out of the mist, and started chasing me. He has a snarl on his face as he reaches out for me. And what's weird, is that he's wearing a pink polka dot dress, and blonde wig. We're running through the mist, and he's closer each time. The last time, he actually touched me. Just as I broke out of the mist, and see the house. Once I reach the porch, I wake up. Then last night, I dreamt of this form, floating in the air. His skin is an awful color, and his eyes have large dark pupils, with fluorescent green ring around them. It's totally frightening."

The others are staring at her oddly.

"See, I knew you wouldn't understand!" She whispered exasperated.

"No, no." Shelly swallows. "Just give us a minute."

"Jess, these are some pretty weird dreams!" Jake exclaimed.

"Tell me about it!" She answered quietly.

"Do you recognize any of them?" Shelly asks.

"Well, I hadn't until yesterday. My mom just bought some insurance from a guy that was introduced by a co-worker. Well, he came to the house yesterday, and when I answered the door, I froze. It was him!"

"It was who?" Shelly looked puzzled.

"The one in the dress." She whispered.

"Wow!" Jake whistled. "You actually recognized him?"

"Yes. And when he introduced himself, we shook hands. I got chills all over. I couldn't wait to pull my hand away." She looked from one to the other. "So what do you think? Could it be intuition? That maybe I'm being warned or something?"

The three of them look at one another, and Jake says, "Maybe your mother shouldn't buy insurance from him. It could have something to do with that." Shrugging his shoulders.

"You might have something there." Dan said thinking.

"But how could I have dreamed of a man I never saw before? And the way I dreamed of him is even scarier."

"You got that right." Shelly whispered. "Wow!"

"Exactly," Dan echoed agreement. "Maybe you should keep an eye on this character. Or maybe even your mom."

"She seems taken with him." She sighed sadly. "He is very nice looking, and friendly. But that doesn't say what kind of a person he is."

"You can't blame your mother, Jess, if she's taken with him. After all she's been alone for over two years now." Shelly said softly.

"I know." Grudgingly agreeing. "So what do you think? Do we have the makings of a mystery?"

"Sounds real possible. And you'd better include me if anything happens." Jake stated matter of factly.

"Now that you all know, I will. But please don't say anything to anybody else. Promise?" She pleaded with them.

"As we said before, scouts honor." Dan said as he covered his heart.

"Please don't think me crazy." She looks sad.

"I need to confide in someone, and who better than my friends?" She finished on a whisper.

Jake gets up, and comes over to her. Taking her hands, he pulls her to her feet, and then sits down, and pulls her onto his lap. "I hope that I'm more than a friend."

She hugged him. "You are." She pulled back, and looked at him. "Does this mean that you would like to be my boyfriend, Jake?" She asks so sweetly.

He smiled back. "Well, I hadn't intended asking like this, but yes, I'd like us to go together." Taking her hand, and kissing it. "Will you be my girlfriend, Jessica?"

She kissed him gently. "I thought you'd never ask," She whispered leaning back into his arms.

"Hey, let's swim a bit, and then maybe I can con my mom into fixing us a snack." Shelly said to lighten the mood.

"Last one in is a rotten egg!" Dan yells as he hit's the water.

"No fair," Shelly squealed as Jake grabbed her, and pulls her back, and jumps in.

"Rotten egg. Rotten egg. Shelly's a rotten egg." Jake teased her.

Shelly picks up the beach ball, and throws it at him. "Just remember, mister, that paybacks are usually a bitch."

Dan swims over to her. "That's alright, Shelly, you can be my rotten egg." Taking her in his arms.

"Does this mean I can say I'm your girl?" She asked sweetly.

He kisses her. "You bet!"

"Here, here," Jake teases. "Enough of that."

"Oh, I see," Shelly pretends anger, "you can do it, but don't let us."

"God, you're gullible." Jake laughs at her.

Shelly kicked water at him. He grabbed her ankle, and pulled her under. She came up sputtering. "Oooh, just you wait!" Looking at Jessie. "Get a grip on your man before I kill him!"

Jessie is laughing at her, and doesn't see Jake reaching for her. Under she went. He grabs her around the waste, and pulls her close. They float to the surface, arm entwined, and lips locked.

Shelly's mom came onto the deck. "Anybody hungry?" As she sets down a tray of finger food.

"You're a mind reader, mother." Shelly laughs in delight.

"I must confess, dear. I heard you." Pointing at the picture. "That's fresh lemonade."

"Great. Thanks, mom."

"Yes, thanks, mom," the others chimed.

She's laughed at them. "You're quite welcome."

They left nothing on the tray, and emptied the pitcher.

Jake rubbed his stomach. "That was good."

"Delicious lemonade." Dan licked his lips.

Jake looked at his watch. "It's ten o'clock, man. What do you think?"

"Any time your ready. Just say the word."

"Well, it's not that I'm in any hurry, but five-thirty is going to roll around pretty quick."

"I should be going too." Jessie stood up.

Thanking Shelly's mom again as they leave.

"I'll call you," Dan shouts as they pull away.

"Bye," Shelly waves as they beep at her.

Jake walks Jessie to the door. Taking her in his arms, "I'll call you when I get back." He kisses her tenderly.

"I might be at Shelly's if you can't get me here."

"Okay." He kisses her again.

"Night," she whispers as he walks away, "don't let the bed bugs bite." Laughing at him.

"What?" He turned to her. "Oh, I got ya." Laughing at her as he gets into his car.

Jessie waves as he pulls away. She leans against the door and touches her lips. Letting herself in, with steps as light as a cloud, she bounds up the stairs. Gathering what she needed to shower, she waltz's down the hall. Touching her lips again, still feeling his kiss. After her shower, she is fluffing her hair, when she hears a car door. She went to the top of the steps, and stood silently.

Dave stepped inside, and took her mom in his arms. "Come with me for the weekend." He kissed her.

"Where?" She asked softly.

"I have a beach house in Monterey." He swings her back and forth. "Come on. You'll have a good time. I promise." Smiling into her eyes.

Smiling back at him. "I'll think about it."

"I can't ask for more than that."

Oh, please don't do it, mother." Jessie whispered.

They stare into one another's eyes. He kissed her forehead. "I'll call you in the morning." He kissed her again. "Good night."

"Good night," as she closes the door.

She started up the stairs, just as Jessie walked to her room. "There you are." She smiled brightly. "I was beginning to wonder about you."

"We went out for dinner." She sighed happily. "You know, sweetie, he is such good company. I haven't enjoyed myself like this in a long time."

"I know, mother." Jessie takes her hands smiling. "That's why you have to take it slow."

Her mother starts laughing. "Listen at you. The daughter chiding the mother." Shaking her head as she came up the stairs.

"Well…" Jessie was at a loss for words.

Squeezing her hands, her mother says, "I have every intention of taking it slow. I suppose you heard what he asked me?"

"Yes I did." She answered truthfully.

"Then you heard my reply. And I will think about it." Touching Jessie's cheek. "I just hope you respect whatever decision I make."

"Yes, mother." As she hugs her.

"Good. Now I'm going to bed."

"Night, mother."

Jessie is far to keyed to go to bed, so she gets the books, and decides to read. Getting a pop, and plopping down in a chair, she just opens a book when the phone rings. "Hello."

"Hey, Jess," Shelly said, "I thought I was spending the night?"

"Ohhh, I'm so sorry," she apologizes. "But you'll have to forgive me if I wasn't myself tonight."

"I understand perfectly." Shelly laughed delightfully. "Can you believe it Jessie?"

"No. I'm still on cloud nine." She pauses. "Is your mom still up?"

"Yes. Why?"

"Why don't you see if she'll let you go ahead and come over. I'm sitting here reading. This stuff is really interesting."

"Hold on and I'll ask." Jessie hears her call to her mother. "Can I go on over to Jessie's? She forgot, and left without me." She paused. "I'm on my way."

"Okay. See you in a few." She lays the phone down and continues to read.

A light tap on the door. "I'll just run this up to your room." Holding out her bag.

"Okay." Jessie smiles at her and goes back to reading.

Shelly plopped down on the couch. "Have you learned anything yet?"

"Well, this says that a lot of times, these sort of dreams are from the unconscious side of yourself. That something has usually happened to trigger it. Like maybe a guilt complex, or fear of something. But if this isn't the case, it can be a warning that something is about to take place, that is out of your control. It says that dreams are meant to bring awareness to you, or whom ever you're dreaming of." She looks up.

"Wow!" Shelly breaths. "That is deep." Getting more comfortable, she asks, "so what do you think? Are you still feeling that this is a warning for your mother?"

Jessie sighs deeply. "I don't know what to think. This is all so crazy. Here, I'll sit by you so we can both read." Pointing at what she had just read. "See what I mean? It's a warning. It has to be." She leaned toward Shelly. "Because I saw a specific person. And... I met that person!"

"Wow! Wow!" Was all Shelly could say.

"I know. It's eerie, isn't it? And you know what else? When he brought her home tonight, he asked her to go to his beach house in Monterey."

"No!" Shelly whispered covering her mouth. "She's not doing it is she?"

"We talked, but I'm not convinced that she won't." She sighs. "He is so attentive of her. I'm afraid she is him a lot."

"How do you feel about that?"

Jessie shrugs her shoulders. "You know, it's not like he's this horrible ogre or anything. And if I hadn't seen him in my dreams, I just might like him." She smiles softly. "He's really good looking, and seems very nice. They do make a cute couple."

"What do you think you should do?" Shelly asked as she gets up. "I'm getting a pop."

"Go ahead. Grab the chip too." Jessie said as she goes back to reading.

"I mean, you must be able to do something. Why else would this happen?" Shelly asks as she sits down.

"I'm not really sure yet, but I think, maybe, we should keep an eye on him."

"How can we do that?" As she opens the chips.

"Well, if you don't mind giving up a little of your time, we can follow them. Just to see what he's like when they're alone."

"Okay. Sure, I can do that. But would your mother want to see him if he was anything but nice?"

"Good point. But mother could miss something, simply because she's taken with him."

"I bet the boys would want to get in on this." Shelly sounded excited. "Judging from their reaction tonight."

"Or else they thought I was plain nuts." Jessie laughed at that thought.

"I don't think so, Jessie. They seemed pretty interested to me. And… Speaking of the boys, I'm still in heaven." She sighs deeply.

"You and me both." They laugh. "How many times have we wished for this?" Jessie sighs. "Finally, after two years."

"Two years." Shelly agreed with a grimace. "I was beginning to give up hope."

"Hope was just about to take wings." Jessie said laughing giddily. "So tell me, Shelly. What did Dan have to say to you?"

"Well. He said that he'd been thinking a lot about me. And he wanted to know if I wanted to make it a done deal?" Shelly laughs at that. "Can you believe it? The way he expresses himself?" wrinkling her nose. "It's kinda cute really."

"I don't have to ask what your answer was." Jessie laughs at her.

"Tell me. What did Jake have to say?"

"He was a little more down to earth." They laughed at that. "He just said that he'd like for us to be regulars."

"I know your answer." Putting her hands together. "Oh yes please. I'll gladly be your girl." Shelly teased her.

Jessie picked up a pillow, and threw it her. Laying the book down. "You don't honestly think they thought me insane or something like that, do you?"

"No," Shelly shakes her head. "To be honest. I think they were intrigued. And I see them getting involved. After all, how often do we get a chance to play sleuth?"

"Yeah, really." Jessie paused and thought. "You know. I wish I could tape my dreams, then you'd know what I'm up against." Pausing again. "It is really strange, that I would dream of him in a dress. He doesn't strike me as the type to like that sort of stuff at all. I mean, this guy is built! Really built, and he definitely likes women. He opens the car door for her. He is real attentive to her." She leaned back and sighs. "I can see why she is so taken with him."

"So exactly what should we do?" Shelly was obviously puzzled.

"I'm just not sure. We'll just have to keep an eye on him."

"Maybe we should wait and see if the boys have any suggestions." Shelly raised her brows.

"I guess you're right."

"This could turn out to be fun. Being a spy, and doing it with the guys of your dreams!" Shelly finished excitedly.

"Boy, you've got it bad!" Jessie laughs.

"Like you don't?" Shelly shot back.

"Okay. Okay. I confess." She laughs. "Isn't it wonderful though?"

Shelly puts both hands together, and looks up. "Thank you." She whispers.

Both girls jump when the phone rings. "Hello," Jessie said softly. Pointing at the phone. "It's Jake," she mouthed to Shelly. Smiling as she leans back into the cushions.

"What are you doing?" Jake asked her softly.

"Sitting here talking to Shelly."

"I can't seem to get myself ready for bed. Is it alright if I come over?"

"Sure. If you don't mind being the odd man out."

"Why's that?"

"Well, Shelly's here, she's spending the night."

"That's okay, 'cause Dan's with me. He's going with us tomorrow, and if I can be tired, so can he." They laugh at that.

"We'll watch for you. Putting the phone down, she squealed. "They are coming over, Shelly! I've got to get dressed." She raced up the stairs. When she came back down, she said, "come on. We'll wait for them on the porch."

Sitting on the swing, Jessie is looking at the heavens, and starts to giggle.

"What's so funny?" Shelly asked looking up.

"Remember the childhood chant? Star light, star bright, first star I see tonight. I wish I may, I wish I might, have this wish

I make tonight." Laughing like a school girl. "Remember that, Shelly?"

"Mmmm. Sometimes I wish I was a little girl again." She said both sadly and softly.

"Can we know what you're talking about?" Jake asks as he sits down by Jessie.

Jessie looked at Shelly. "Should we tell them?"

Dan pulls Shelly to her feet, and sits down, pulling her onto his lap.

"Well I don't know." She paused. "They'll just laugh at us."

"Maybe we will." Dan squeezed her.

"We were talking about being girls again." Shelly whispered.

"Remember, star light, star bright? That's all we were talking about." Jessie said simply.

"If you say so." Jake said unbelieving.

"Honest." Shelly said in defense.

"But we do have something more pressing to talk about." Jessie said quietly. She sat in silence for a moment. Then sighing deeply, she leaned into him. "We were talking about my dreams when you called. Trying to decide how we can get to the bottom of them. After reading that book I got at the library, it's clear these dreams have a meaning. And we think it's a warning."

"Could be, but of what?" Jake muses.

Jessie shrugs her shoulders. "It doesn't make sense. I see this man in a dress, and a wig. He's chasing me. It seems he's trying to get me. Then out of the blue, here comes this man, and he enters my mothers life. At least it looks like him." She sighs. "So Shelly and I think we should keep an eye on him."

"Wait a minute. Wait a minute!" Jake holds up his hands. "You haven't the slightest clue about this guy! You could be getting into something way over your heads."

"Well… We though maybe we could get you two to help us." She pleaded. "Wouldn't you like to play sleuth?" She asks sweetly.

Jake and Dan look at one another. "Promise you won't do anything until we get back." Jake turned her face to his. He looked square into her eyes. "Promise!"

"Promise," she sighed unconvincingly. He squeezed her. "Alright!" She laughs. "I promise."

"Good. That's better." He relaxed.

"How about some ice cream?" Dan asked Shelly.

"Okay," Shelly and Jessie say together.

"Your mom won't care if you leave?" Dan asked Jessie.

"Not just to go to the Dairy Queen."

A group of their friends was there and they hung around for a bit. Jessie and Shelly were talking with a close friend, Jenny. Jake came over and touched her arm.

"It's one o'clock. We'd best get back."

"You're probably right." Turning to Jenny. "I'll talk to you later. Maybe we'll see you at the beach tomorrow." Jessie waves as they pull away.

Jake follows her into the house. He takes her into his arms, and kisses her passionately. "Can I tell you something?" In a husky voice.

She shakes her head yes, while she held her breath.

"I love you," He whispered as he kissed her again.

"I love you too," against his lips.

He kissed her passionately again, and she melted into him. "I think I should go." Kissing her again.

"Yeah." Was all she could say. They walk to the door. "I'll see you tomorrow?"

"I don't know. It depends on what time we get back." He kissed her, and leaping from the porch, "I'll call you."

As they pulled away, Jessie wheeled, and grabbed Shelly's hands. "He told me he loved me, Shelly. And I couldn't breathe. Then he said, he'd better go, but I didn't want him to." All in one breath, and she sighs. "Maybe it was for the best, huh? Otherwise we might have had sex."

"That day will come you know." Shelly stated.

"What am I going to do?" Jessie plopped down on the swing.

"Follow you heart." They looked long at one another. "I will."

"Will you?" Jessie frowned.

"Yes. At least I think so." Sighing.

"He's never kissed me like that before, Shelly. It was wonderful. You know what? I don't think I need to wish upon that star." She laughs giddily.

Shelly hugs her. "We're pretty lucky aren't we?"

"Yes we are." Jessie stands. "We should turn in ourselves."

As they prepare for bed, she looks at Shelly. Clearing her throat, "if I holler out in the night, don't be frightened. It means I'm having that dream again. I'll wake up. I always do." Pulling down the covers. "You'll be alright won't you?"

"I hope so." Shelly answered truthfully.

Jessie lay looking at the ceiling. "I don't think I can sleep."

"You should try." Shelly said gently.

Jessie sighed. "You're right. It's just that I love him so much.""Mmmm." Shelly closed her eyes.

"Night, Shelly."

"Night."

Rolling onto her side, Jessie closes her eyes.

She's running, but there's no mist this time. She feels the desperate need to find her house. She glances back, but sees nothing, yet she feels his presence. She feels a different fear this time. She must get home. She searches for the house, but can't find it. She can feel her heart skipping beats, as she searches frantically for her house. Where is it? Oh please, God. Please let me find it, as she turns and circles. She feels the chills run up and down her spine, as she hears a gurgle. Glancing back, she sees that form appear, dark and menacing. Sneering at her, and staring with those ugly black, and fluorescent green eyes. As it slowly moves closer to her, she turns, and tries to run faster. Run, run. She tells herself. Then she does what she has been trying so hard not to do. She stumbles and loses her balance. As she is going down, she whispers in horror, "no! No!" And she hit's the ground, and rolls over. The form is hanging over her, making gurgling sounds, and hissing at her. It would drift up, and then drop back down, hissing at her, and sneering. Dripping goo from it's mouth, and falling onto her face as those eyes stared a hole into her being. She scoots backwards, and getting to her feet, turns and runs. She sees her mother standing on the porch, with her arms outstretched, and she runs into them. As her mothers arms encircle her, and pull her close, she wakes up.

Shelly is sitting on the edge of her bed when she opens her eyes. "Are you okay?" Taking her hands and holding them to still the trembling. They are covered with sweat. "We really must do something." She whispered. Her eyes as wide as silver dollar. "I'll be right back." She goes into the bathroom, and gets a wash cloth, and wets it with cold water. She comes back, and wipes Jessie's face off, and sits by her again.

"I'm sorry you had to see this." Jessie whispered hoarsely.

"That's okay, Jess. At least now I have an idea of what you go through." Shelly sighs. "We are going to have to find out, one way or another, why this is happening. Is he such a monster?"

"It wasn't him." Jessie shuddered.

"Then who was it?"

"The other one that I told you about. With the grey skin, and evil looking eyes." She shuddered again. "I was really terrified of it, Shelly. I believe it is worse, much worse than the other man I see." She shakes her head. "I don't know. I just can't explain it. I do know that I have this immense fear of it. And," she made a face, "it was dripping this goo all over my face. It seemed to know that I was terrified to death." She sighs. "I think this one is very, very evil."

"Are you going to be okay?" Shelly asked as she got back into bed.

"There usually isn't a repeat the same night." She lays back on her bed, and does something she rarely ever does. She closed her eyes and prayed. For understanding, and the strength to endure this nightmare that has entered her life.

****

II

The next thing Jessie knows, is that it's bright outside, and the birds are chirping. As if to say, wake up you sleepy head. She looks over at Shelly, and she too has been awakened by the chirping of the birds. Stretching, Jessie pushed back the covers, and stands up, stretching again.

"Well," as she makes the bed. "What are we doing today?"

"I think we should talk." Shelly answers her, studying her face.

"Probably so, but first, let's see if mother is still here. Maybe I can talk her into breakfast out. Waving her brows at Shelly, who just shakes her head.

"Okay," Shelly smiles. "Jessie," laying her hand on her arm, "I don't want you feeling embarrassment about last night. You know that you are like a sister to me, and I'll always be there for you."

Jessie stared at her for a moment, and then hugs her. "I know that."

Carol is sitting at the table reading the morning paper. She looks up when they walk into the kitchen. "Good morning." She smiles.

"Good morning, mother." Jessie kisses her cheek.

"Morning," Shelly echoes.

"Have you eaten yet?" Jessie asks sweetly.

"No. I'm just enjoying my coffee." Carol gives her a suspicious look. "Why?"

"Oh, no particular reason, other than, maybe we can eat out." As she smiles sweetly at her.

Carol laughs. "I guess we could do that."

"I'll buy, if you want me to." Jessie offers.

"That won't be necessary." As she stands up looking at Jessie she asks, "I take it you had a quiet night?" She rinsed out her cup.

"Uh-huh." Looking at Shelly, and imploring her not to say anything.

"That's good to hear." She reached for her purse. "Are we ready?"

Jessie reached for her mom's hand, and squeezed it gently.

Carol looked at her oddly, but didn't say anything.

They talk about their day with the fellas, and were enjoying themselves, when out of the blue, Jessie said, "so, mother. Tell me. How is it with your new found friend?" She smiles coyly at Shelly. "I think she's in love." Waving her brows.

"Knock it off." Carol laughs. Her face getting a little flushed.

"But I really want to know." Jessie said very sweetly. "I'll be good. I promise." She crossed her heart, smiling at Shelly.

Her mom was quiet for a moment. "I don't want you to be upset over this."

"Please, mother. I'm not a little girl anymore. If you care for this man, then don't worry about my feelings." She smiles sadly. "Father has been gone for two years now. I've gotten on with my life, as I think you should."

"But?" Carol questioned. "I hear a but in there."

Jessie looked at Shelly. "I just hope he shares your emotions, that's all."

"I'm sure he does." She hesitates. "I think I would like to go to his beach house." She sighs deeply. "It has been such a long time since a man has been able to even get close enough for a date. And Dave has a personality to die for." She laughed. "You should see the looks I get when I go out with him."

"Interesting choice of words, mother." Jessie said sarcastically. "And if you want to go with him, do it. I think you've been alone long enough. Don't you?"

"He's going to call me after a bit. I'll know for sure by then what I'm going to do." Looking at both girls. "What are you planning for today?"

"I got some books from the library, and we're going to do some serious reading. Since the boys went with Jake's dad, and won't be back until late."

"What kind of books?"

"Oh. They're about dreams, intuitions, that sort of thing." She answered carelessly.

"Because of your dreams?" Raising a brow. "Are they as bad?"

"I guess you could say that." Jessie hedged.

"Are we ready." Carol picked up her purse. "I don't want to miss Dave's call."

"Sure." Jessie laughed at her.

"Don't start." Her mother warned.

"What?" Spreading her hands in innocence.

They hadn't been home long when the phone rang. Jessie picked it up. "Hello."

"Hi," Dave said cheerfully. "Is Carol there?"

"One moment, please." She turns and holds out the phone. "Guess who?" She teased.

Carol snatches the phone from Jessie, giving her a look.

Jessie laughs at her as she runs up to her room. She feels Shelly staring at her, and looks up.

"Do you really not mind that your mom is getting serious about him?" She looks very puzzled.

"It's not that." She sits on her bed. "I see this man in my nightmares, the next thing I know, he's knocking on my door, and then dating my mother! Go figure! But nothing compares to the terror I feel when I dream of the other! You know, Shelly. Maybe whatever, or whomever that thing is, is the real danger. Just say that Dave is acquainted with it, and is being used to get us close to it also. Get us to trust Dave, and then move in…" She didn't finish the sentence.

"For what?" Shelly spreads her hands.

Jessie cleared her throat. "The kill!"

"Oh don't say that!" Shelly looked horrified.

"Relax," Jessie laughs at her. "That's just a figure of speech."

"Not a very good choice of words, Jessie." Shelly shot her a look of distaste.

"Sorry." Jessie apologized.

"I'm getting chills." Shelly hugs herself. "Do know who introduced them?"

"A lady that works with my mother at her office."

"Do you know her?"

"Not really. I met her once at a picnic. I know that mother doesn't particularly like her. She said often that she gives her the willies." Her eyes lock with Shelly's. "Hum. I wonder?"

"What? What?" Shelly's on the edge of the bed now. "What are you thinking?"

"Well, this may sound crazy, but just suppose that she is that evil, grey colored thing, with the ugly eyes, that I dream of. Don't the eyes always show madness?"

"That's what they say. I know that they certainly have a look about them." She shuddered.

"Mother has said different times that this lady doesn't like her, and that she stays out of her way. As much as possible that is."

"The more you talk, the less I like her, and I don't even know the lady!" Shelly made a face. "So what do we do?"

"Let's find out as much about her as we can." She sighs. "I only hope this guy is legit with my mom. She has been through enough."

"I know," Shelly answered sadly. "So how do we find out about her?"

"Mother." Jessie answered simply. "We'll ask just how she came to meet him. And when she tells us about the woman at work, we'll ask her name. Then we'll figure out where to go from there."

Carol taps on the door. "I'm going to pack a bag, Jessie. I decided to go with him. And I don't want you worrying about me." She smiled. "I'll be just fine." Taking Jessie's hand. "Be happy for me, dear. I'm getting a second chance."

Jessie hugged her. "You do whatever you feel you have to, mother. I understand." Looking over her mom's shoulder, and winking at Shelly. "So, exactly how did you two meet anyhow?"

"You know that woman I've told you about? The one that gives me the creeps. Alice is her name. Anyhow, she asked me if we had enough insurance on us. Especially me. So that you wouldn't have to be struggling, and hurting at the same time. I never thought about it, but she had a point. She made me aware of what could happen to you if I had an accident, or something like that."

"Why would she show so much interest in you all of a sudden?" Jessie asked, clearly puzzled by it. "I mean, she doesn't even like you. For what reason you never understood, and then she talks of protecting us?" "I know. Those were my thoughts exactly, but I let her talk me into meeting this insurance man. And you know the rest." She sighs.

"So you like him, huh?" Jessie teased to lighten the mood.

"Yes, I do." She smiled softly. "Now I'd better get ready. He'll be here, and I won't have my bag packed."

Jessie pushes her. "Hurry. Hurry, mother." Laughing at her.

Jessie motions Shelly down stairs. In the kitchen she whispers excitedly, "can you believe this, Shelly?"

"What are you talking about?" She was clearly puzzled by Jessie's remark.

"Don't you see? That's it! That's why I'm having these dreams."

"What's it?" Shelly spreads her hands, exasperated.

"Why I'm having these dreams, Shelly, could be, that woman's intentions against my mother. I'll just bet you this is a warning! Think about this for a minute. What if she told Dave about my mom being alone? That her husband was dead. What if she tried to match make with not so good intentions?"

"No!" Shelly exclaimed. "That's not even funny!"

"I doubt that it's meant to be." Jessie said in anger.

"How do we find out? I mean, we can't just come right out and ask Dave if this person sent him to do a dirty deed." Shelly said, all in one breath. Then her eyes widened, covering her mouth, she cried, "what if he is luring your mom? Pretending to be falling for her?""Now you're getting the picture, Shelly." She plopped down in a chair. Looking from Shelly, out the window, she felt a sadness she hadn't felt for a long time. "If we're right, I sure hope Dave has a change of heart after he gets to know my mom. She certainly has been smitten. Don't you agree?"

"Yes, I would say that." Shelly smiles. "I'll pray for her." She whispered.

"How am I to find out about this woman without arousing my mom's suspicions?" Jessie sounded hopeless. "I'll ask her. I have no possible reason for wanting to know her full name, other than being curious." Shelly offered.

"Curious about what?" Carol asked as she came down the stairs.

"I was just wondering what that woman's full name is, that wanted you to meet Dave?" Shelly smiled sweetly, "that's all."

"Alice Watson." She laughed. "I wouldn't be too curious about her. She's weird."

"So you've said." Jessie said sarcastically. "Then, if I may, why did you agree to meeting Dave?"

"To be honest, she made sense in what she said. What, with the cost of burials and all, she gave me a minute to pause."

"So she told you about this insurance person, and proceeded to introduce you." Jessie finished for her.

"Yes. And I agreed to it." She paused. "I had no idea we'd click like we did.""You certainly seem to do that alright!" Jessie laughed.

They jumped when Dave knocked on the door. They all laughed.

"What's so funny?" Dave asked, as Carol let him in.

"You scared up." Jessie said frankly.

"I what?" He asked bewildered. "Gee, I'm sorry. I didn't mean to."

Carol laughed at him. "We were so into our conversation, that we didn't hear you come onto the porch. When you knocked, we all jumped."

"Well, the next time, I'll make some noise to let you know I'm here."

They all laughed at that.

He turned to Carol. "Are you ready?"

Picking up her bag, she gave Jessie a hug and a kiss. "Be have," she whispered in her ear.

"Always. And you have a good time." Looking at Dave, she smiles sweetly. "Take good care of her, she's all I've got."

"I'll guard her with my life." He teased as he took her arm.

As they walked to the car, he said, "I think you're daughter is starting to like me." Smiling broadly.

Looking over her shoulder, and waving, "I think you might be right."

"Bye," Jessie said as they pulled away. Turning to Shelly and saying, "now we have to figure out the best way to do this."

"Maybe someone who works with your mom would be able to tell you something."

"Donna would. Her and mother are good friends." She picked up the phone. After three rings, the answering machine kicked on. "Donna, this is Jessica. There is nothing wrong, but, could you please give me a call when you have time? Thanks."

"Now what?" Shelly sounded very disappointed. "Why don't we forget about this for now?" Jessie said. "Let's see if some of the girls want to go to the beach."

"Know what?" Shelly brightened up. "That's a great idea."

They made a few calls to their friends, put on their bathing suits, and out the door they went. Leaving, for the moment, the dreams behind them. Some of their friends were already swimming when they got there. "Hurry. The water is great." Someone called out. They run for the water.

As they lay tanning, later, Jessie asks innocently, "so, who's ready for college?" "College? Ugh! Jenny answered.

"Double that!" Pam agreed vehemently.

"Oh, come on you guys." Jessie chides them. "It can't be all that bad."

"You… Might not think so," Lynn said sarcastically, "but for the rest of us. Ugh!"

Jessie laughs at them. "Okay. So I'll change the subject." She sits up. "Guess what?" She looks like that cat that ate the mouse.

The others look at her, and Jenny says, "go on. I can tell you're dying to spill the beans." Everybody laughs.

"Maybe for that, I won't tell you now." Jessie pouts, and looks away.

They look at one another. "Not tell us?!"

"Jessie!" Pam threatens.

"Oh, alright." Grinning from ear to ear. "Jake asked me to be his girlfriend."

The others sit up squealing. "You lucky bitch!" Lynn said vehemently.

"Tell us everything." Jenny breathed out.

"Where were you guys yesterday? We spent the whole day here, and I never saw a one of you."

"I had to work." Pam said.

"Me too," Lynn said. "And why are you changing the subject?"

"Come on, Jessie." Pam pleaded. "I could just strangle you when you do this!"

"And I had a family reunion to go to." Jenny said. "Now talk!"

"There's not really much to tell." She smiled, and sighed. She was deliberately toying with them. "We just spent the entire day together! First the beach, then to Shelly's house, and then mine."

Lynn looked at Shelly. "I suppose you were with the other one?"

Shelly just smiled at her. Knowing it was eating her up inside.

"Bitch!" Lynn said again.

"And he told me he loved me." Jessie sighed deeply.

Jenny hugged her. "You're so lucky."

"Thanks," Jessie smiled warmly at her.

"And I can tell that everything went well for you too." Lynn spat at Shelly. "You have this glow about you."

"You could say that," Shelly's voice bubbled. "He wants to make it a done deal."

The others laughed. "He wouldn't put it that way." Lynn snapped.

"You're just jealous," Shelly smiled sweetly at her.

"You're right, I am." Lynn responded. "They're the two most gorgeous guys in town. And who gets them?" She pouts. "Not me!"

"Lighten up, will you, Lynn." Pam said in distaste.

"I'm just joking," Lynn replied a little sheepishly.

"Anyhow, I said yes." Shelly finished charmingly. "Quickly, I might add."

They all laugh. Lynn gives a dark squall at everybody. "I answered pretty darn quick too," Jessie echoed, Looking right at Lynn, and smiling.

"I just might be saying the same thing real soon." Pam smiled broadly.

Lynn leveled a look on her too, and said, "don't tell me Eric has become amorous too!" She fell back in the sand. "This is so unfair."

Jenny pats her on the arm. "Perk up, Lynn. Our day will come."

"I doubt that." She pouted.

"Keep thinking like that, and it probably won't." Jessie said frankly.

"That's Jess. Always giving advice." Lynn looked at her. "Who gives you advice when you need it? Or don't you ever?"

Jessie sensed her being sarcastic, and smiling very sweetly, said, "that's what mothers are for."

"So you're going off to college, with a boyfriend? Do you think that's wise?" Jenny asked Jessie.

"Actually, I do." She paused to be sure she used the right words. "I'm going there to get an education, not check out the boys. They'll know I have a boyfriend, and I can concentrate on my classes."

"That's Jessie," Shelly teased. "All business."

"And she'll probably go the further, of all us girls." Jenny said, quite frankly.

"What about you and Mike? What's up there?" Jessie asked Jenny.

"Not much." She shrugs her shoulder. "We'll be going to the same school, but, I don't know how that's going to work out. We'll just have to wait and see." She stood up. "It's time for another swim."

They all raced for the water.

Lynn pointed to the shore. "Speaking of the devil."

"Don't let him hear you call him that, Lynn. Or he just might be."

The others looked at her oddly, but didn't say anything.

"He's a little on the rough side sometimes." Jenny said when she noticed their looks.

"Oh," was all that was said. Jessica looked at her, and made a mental note to ask Jake about him. Maybe he could use some help.

He swam over to Jenny. "I tried to call you. I thought you might come here with me?"

"Jessie called me early this morning. With me working at the hospital, I haven't seen much of them this summer. So I agreed to meet them here."

"That's cool. What are you doing tonight?"

"I hadn't planned anything. What's up?"

"Do you want to go to a party?"

"Where?" Jenny hedged.

"At Tim's. He's having a bonfire."

"I don't know. Let me think about it."

"Come on," Mike splashed her, "we'll have a good time."

"Let me think about it," she pleaded.

"Sure. Just don't take all night."

"Mike, you're being paged." Jessie pointed to the beach.

"Come on in," he shouted.

"They hit the water on the run, and the girls scramble to get out of their way. Pam got dunked, and came up swinging at the one who dunked her. He ducked under, and came up beneath her, and lifted her out of the water.

"Eric," she squealed, "you put me down," laughing as he did so, by tossing her over his head. She came up sputtering, and he grabbed her again. Taking her n his arms, he held her close.

"What," she laughs nervously. "Why are you looking at me like that?"

"No particular reason." Eric replies, still staring at her.

"Well, don't. You're making me nervous."

"Come with me tonight?" He swims around her. Splashing her face.

"To Tim's party. I'll behave, I promise."

"I bet you will!" She smirked.

He dunked her again. "Alright. I'll come with you." She sputtered as she came up.

"Good." Was all he replied.

Jenny swims over to her and whispers. "Are you going Pam?"

"I guess so. Are you?"

"Since you are I will. I just didn't want to go alone." She swam back to Mike. "I'll go with you tonight, but you have to be good."

Mike said to Lynn. "Tim's been trying to get ahold of you.""Really? Why?" Lynn snapped.

"He's having a bonfire tonight. Give him a call when you get home."

"Who are you to give me orders, Mike?" She smarted off at him.

He gave her a dark look and turned back to Jenny and ignored her.

"Pam, are you going tonight?" Lynn asker her.

"To the party you mean? Yeah, I guess so.""I guess it will be fun. That is if he doesn't have those losers from across town there. Every time they show up things get out of hand." Lynn pouted.

"I know. That's the only reason I hesitated. Eric is such fun, but when they show up it's like they all change."

"Exactly!" Lynn agreed. "Oh well, if they show up we'll just leave. I won't be a part of their drinking anymore."

"Me either. But the one who gets the worst is Mike." Pam whispered sadly.

"Poor Jenny." Lynn whispered back.

Jessie says to Shelly, "I don't know about you, but I'm ready to go home. I'm hungry."

"I'm kinda hungry myself." Shelly agreed with her.

"Hey, guys. We're going to head on home." Jessie patted her stomach and laughed. "I'm hungry."

"Okay, Jessie. I'll give you a call." Jenny hugs her. "I really meant it when I said good luck with Jake."

"I wish others felt that way." Rolling her eyes toward Lynn. "She'll lighten up. You know she's always had this thing for him."

"Yes, I know." She waves to the others as she leaves the water.

"Can you believe the way Lynn acted today?" Shelly asked in anger.

"Actually I can." Jessie stated. "You know she has always been the jealous one of the bunch and that she has liked, at one time or another, both our fellas."

"Yeah I know. You don't think she'll try anything do you?"

Jessie shrugged her shoulders. "Who knows what jealousy will do."

"You can bet I'll be watching her! I finally get the man of my dreams and I'm not about to let the likes of her take him away." Shelly said very defiantly.

"I hardly think you have to worry about that." Jessie laughed at her. "The boys have made it clear who they want and that's good enough for me."

"I guess you're right." Shelly sighed. "She just worries me that's all."

"Well, Shelly, look at it this way. Love conquers all."

"I guess we'll see won't we."

"Oh come on, Shelly." Jessie punches her shoulder. "If Dan wanted her he's had every opportunity to do so."

"He probably has!" Shelly spat.

"That was mean!" Jessie chided.

"Well it's true!" She laughed. "I'm sorry. You're not supposed to talk about friends that way are you? But she makes me so mad!"

"Who doesn't she make mad?" They laughed together. "That was so mean." Still laughing.

"Well the truth will set you free." Shelly said feeling much better now. "You can drop me off at home, Jess, so I can get a shower. I'll get my bag later."

"Okay," as she sighs deeply.

"What was that for?"

"What?"

"That deep sigh."

Jessie smiles at her. "I was thinking about Jake. I hope he calls this evening."

"Ummm, me too." She answered dreamily.

"I don't want to go to that party either. I get tired of those red necks trying to paw me." She screwed her face in distaste.

"Jake might do something about that now."

"I'll probably see you later."

"Let's hope." She toots and waves as she pulls away.

As she lets herself in she hears the phone ringing and runs to answer it. "Hello."

"I was ready to hang up. Where were you?" Her mother asked.

"At the beach with the girls. I just came in."

"I just wanted to let you know that I am spending the night up here. Ill be home sometime tomorrow evening."

"Okay, mother."

"Will you be alright?"

"Of course I will, silly. After all, mother, I am nineteen." She laughs.

"That's so old, Jessica." Her mother laughed at her.

"Really, mother. I'll be fine." Clearing her throat she asks, "so things are going well?"

"Oh yes! Very well." She sighed. "I'm having a wonderful time."

"That's good." Jessie pauses for a moment. "Guess what?"

"What?" Her mother sounded a little apprehensive.

"I forgot to tell you something this morning." She paused again.

"Well," her mother said a little impatiently. "What is it?"

"Jake asked me to be his girl last night!"

"Why, sweetie, that's wonderful! But you just take it slow for a while."

"Oh, mother," Jessie laughed at her, "we've been seeing one another for two years now!"

"I know. I know, but kids can be so impulsive these days." She sighed. "Well, dear, I'm getting off here. We're going to get a bite to eat and then go to a party."

"Ooooh, a party." Jessie teased her.

"Yes a party." Her mother laughs back. "See you tomorrow evening."

"Okay. Love you, mother."

"Lover you too, sweetie. Bye."

Smiling as she hangs up the phone shaking her head. She runs up the steps to get a shower and then find something to eat. As the is about to climb into the shower she hears the phone ring. "Drat it," she muttered. "They'll just have to call back."

Fluffing her hair as she comes back down stairs, she heads straight for the kitchen. Rubbing her stomach as it growls again. As she reaches for the handle on the fridge the phone rings again. Sighing she picks it up. "Hello."

"Hello. Jessica? This is Donna. You called earlier?"

"Yes I did. I wanted to ask you about a woman you work with."

"Alice Watson."

"Oh that one!" She sighed. "Well, lets just say that you don't know about her, except that she is strange and unsociable. She certainly doesn't let anyone get close enough to get to know her."

"I see," Jessie sighed. "That doesn't help me at all."

"If I may ask, why are you interested in this woman?" Donna sounded concerned.

Jessie cleared her throat. "Well, it's rather an odd story." She hesitated not knowing what to say or just how much. "Mother has told me a little about her, but not enough to really understand what she is like. It has to do with…"

"If it's about your dreams, Jessica, you tan talk to me. Your mother and I are close and she told me everything."

"Oh!" Jessie said very surprised.

"She is just concerned for your well being, dear. Now talk to me."

"You have to promise me first, that what I'm about to tell you won't get to my mother. Not yet anyhow."

"This sounds serious." She paused for a moment. "Alright, dear. You can talk to me."

"Well you know abut the man in my dreams then, the one wearing the dress and wig?"

"Yes. Carol told me."

"What I didn't tell her, was that the man I saw is with her right now."

"What?" Donna sounded very alarmed. "Are you sure?"

"Yes, he is. When he came to the house the other day, you could have knocked me over with your little finger. I simply froze in my tracks when I saw him."

"And your mother doesn't know this?"

"No. I didn't tell her. At first I didn't have the opportunity, then mother started seeing him and I was afraid to say anything."

"I see. All I know is that Alice was talking to your mother about insurance. It's true we don't have good coverage, but we thought it strange that she would all of a sudden be concerned with your mom's welfare."

"That's my feelings exactly. So you really don't know much about her either? What about Dave?"

"No, I'm sorry. I never met him, but you're right. You mom is seeing him. And from what she tells me she likes him a lot. As for Alice, she has been distant since the day she started here."

"When was that?"

"About two years ago. I think it was just before your dad died." She paused. "Yes, that's when it was. You'd best do what we all do and that's leave her alone. She's really nasty. Especially to your mother."

"I wonder why?"

"I wish I knew what to tell you, honey, but that one is truly a mystery."

"Do you know where she lives?"

"Out by the lake somewhere. It sits off by itself and she has never invited any of us out." "Rather fitting huh? That she should be off by herself?"

"You listen to me, Jessica, and don't plan on doing anything stupid! Like going out there or trying to get to know her. She's best just left alone." She said sternly.

"No, no. I'm not going to do anything like that." Jessie assured her.

"Well that's good, dear, because you'd come out the loser." She emphasized. "I'd hate to see you get into trouble with her. I just can't emphasize enough, Jessica, how I feel about this woman."

"I'll remember that." Jessie laughed nervously.

"If you need anything at all, Jessica. Just call me. I'll help you out all I can." "I will. Thanks, Donna."

"You're quite welcome, dear."

As she hangs up she stands there pondering all that was told to her. I think mother is in trouble. And I can't sit back and let that happen. But what can I do? She asks herself. There must be something. The phone rings and she jumps.

"Hello, Jess," Jake said.

"Jake!" She breathed. "Where are you?"

He laughs at her reaction. "On my way home. You sound like you're happy to hear from me."

"I am," she said softly. She gets into the fridge and gets out the lunch meat.

"What are you doing?"

"I'm going to fix a sandwich. I'm starving."

"I wanted to let you know I should be home around eight. I'll get cleaned up and then be over."

"Okay. I'll be waiting."

"Well, I'll see you then."

"Bye." She said dreamily. She was standing there holding the phone when it rang again. "Hello."

"Did you get a call?" Shelly asked excitedly.

"Yes I did. Are you coming over?"

"I'll ask Dan. Maybe we can order pizza and watch a movie."

"We could always suggest a late show."

"I like the idea of pizza and a movie at your house. It's more romantic."

"You're right. What was I thinking?" Jessie laughs. "We'll find something on TV so we can cuddle."

Now you're talking." Shelly laughed at her. "So I'll probably see you later."

"Bye, Shelly. She makes her sandwich and taking the phone goes out to sit on the porch. Just as she lays the phone sown it rings. "Hello."

"Hi, Jessie. What are you doing?" Jenny asked her.

"Sitting on the porch eating a sandwich. What's up?"

"Why don't you and Shelly come to Tim's? The party is great!"

"No red necks yet huh?" Jessie laughed.

"No, not yet anyway. So what do you think? Will you be over?"

"I'd better not. Jake just called me, and he'll be here around nine. So I had better wait and see what he wants to do."

"If you change your mind, I'll be here." She sounded very disappointed.

"Okay, Jenny. I'll talk to you later. Bye."

She was still sitting on the porch when Jake pulled up. She smiled as he sat down beside her. "Hi," smiling into his eyes.

He kissed her deeply.

"I missed you too." She whispered against his lips.

He blushed. "Yeah," was all he said.

"So how was the trip?" She leaned against him.

"They're always long," as he pulled her close. "But this time I had something to occupy my mind."

"I'm glad." She kissed him softly.

"Are we doing anything tonight?"

She laid her head on his shoulder, "why don't we order pizza and see what's on TV?"

"I was hoping you wouldn't want to go to Tim's party." He sighed in relief.

"I was hoping the same thing." She turned in his arms and placing her hands on his face, "I would just like to spend the evening with you."

He pulled her tight and kissed her. "Ditto." He breathed.

She snuggled close. "What do you know about Mike?"

"Mike? Why?" Jake asked in puzzled tones.

"Shelly and I went to the beach with the girls and Lynn said something sarcastic about Mike." She paused. "Jenny made a remark about him being ruff. I just wondered what she meant."

Jake cleared his throat. "Well… Mike had it kind of rough growing up. Before his mom and dad split up, he had to watch her get hit all the time. He even took a few punches himself." He sighed deeply. "That makes for a troubled man."

"I didn't know it was that bad."

"Dan and I try to help him, but I don't know if it's doing any good. Especially when he hangs with that crowd from across town. Drinking and partying all the time."

"Jenny likes him, but I don't see her putting up with anything abusive. I know I wouldn't."

"Are you hungry? We can order that pizza."

"A little. But I can always eat pizza." She laughed at that. "Maybe you'd better order two." "Why's that?"

"In case Dan and Shelly shows up." She hands him the phone.

He pulls her to her feet. "Let's go inside."

"Okay." She smiled sweetly.

"What do you want on you pizza?"

"Whatever. I'm not hard to please." She plops onto the couch. "I hope there is something good on TV."

He sits down and pulls her onto his lap. She's laughing when that see car lights. "Guess who?"

"I hope you don't mind?" She asked timidly.

"Not at all. The nights still young." He bends her over and kisses her.

"Aw-hah! We caught you." Shelly teased.

"Jake ordered pizza, and I'm trying to find out what's on TV. Maybe Pay Per View."

"Is that what you were doing?" Dan asked innocently.

They all laughed at that.

Dan sits down and pulls Shelly onto his lap.

"What's everybody drinking?" Jessie stood up. "I'll bring the dip and chips too."

"Pepsi," They all echoed.

"Okay!" Jessie laughed.

"What are we watching?" Dan asked as she came back into the room.

"I don't know." Jake reached for the control. "Let's see what's on."

"Hey, the sixth Sense is on Pay Per View." Jessie said looking at Shelly and trying to send a message with her eyes. Cuddle, Shelly, Cuddle.

"I see dead people." Jake whispered into her ear. "Aaah," as he bit her neck.

"Stop it." she squealed, pushing him away.

"Here's one we can watch." Turning to her and raising his arms in gesture, "I am count Dracula," Rolling his tongue, "and I want to drink you blood." As he pounced on her.

Squealing as she hits him with closed fists. He pretends to be sucking her blood.

"You are in my power." Jake kissed her ear. "You will come with me. And I will feast n you forever." He bites her neck again.

She's laughing so hard, she can't defend herself anymore.

A knock on the door saved her. "Pizza's here," She breathed out.

"Dratted timing," he teased.

"Blissful timing," she laughs back as he answers the door.

"Dig in everybody," as he sets it down.

"Mmm, smells like heaven." Shelly said as she sniffs the air.

"Amen." Dan agreed as he handed her a piece.

"Let me pay for one of these." Dan offered.

"You can catch the next time."

"So what are we watching? Does everybody like Ashley Judd?" Jessie looks from one to the other of the fellas.

"Yeah, she's okay." Jake said.

"No. Wait a minute!" As she saw something that caught her eye. "Let's watch Stir of Echoes with Kevin Bacon."

"Yeah, let's watch that one." Shelly was quick to agree.

"Okay with you two?" Jessie asked again.

"Whatever you girls want." They said together.

"Good. I've been wanting to see this." Jessie sighed as she looked at Shelly.

They finished the pizza as they watched the movie in silence. At one point, the girls were so into it, that when Jake growled they both jumped. He laughed at them and Jessie slugged him.

Jake grabbed her arms and pushed her over. And leaning over her said, "I'm going to bite you throat," rolling his tongue as he lowered his mouth to her neck.

"Jake, I want to watch this movie." She pleaded with him.

"To bad," he teased as he gnawed at her.

"Come on. It's almost over." She squealed as he bit again.

He let her up. "Alright. I'll behave."

"You'd better." She punched his arm.

Leaning back and pulling her with him, they watch the rest of the movie in silence.

When it was over Dan said, "that was different."

"That was good!" Shelly said back to him.

"Girls just like things that scare them." Jake said. "Not always." Shelly defended them.

"Just most of the time," Dan said as he turned to her. "Shelly, Shelly, I want to bite you throat. I want to suck you blood." Raising his arms and slowly moving to her.

She squealed and tried to run, but he caught her and they fell to the floor. They rustled as he tried to bite her neck.

"You could help me," she pleaded with Jessie.

"Not me. Fight your own battles." Laughing at her.

"Thanks," she said as he bit her. She squealed, pushing at him.

"Any time," Jessie replied just as Jake pounced on her and the battle was on.

The play ended in kissing and as both couples sat up, Jessie reached for the remote. "I think we can shut this off now."

Jake pulled her into his arms and kissed her again. "I love you," he whispered into her ear.

"I love you too." Smiling into his eyes.

Dan cleared his throat. "So what do you think, man? Should we head for home?"

"No," Jessie whispered.

"No?" Jake repeated. He looks deep into her eyes.

Shaking her head as she pushes her hair back. "Not yet anyhow."

He kissed her fingers as he looked into her eyes.

"Shelly, help me carry this stuff to the kitchen." Jessie implored her with her eyes.

Once they were in the kitchen out of ear shot from the fellas she asked, "so what do you think?"

"About what?" Shelly played dumb.

"Do you want to stay here?" Studying her face. "You can use the spare bedroom."

"I don't know." Looking at Jessie nervously. "Are you…?"

"I think I am." Taking a deep breath. "I think I'm ready to find out about being a woman."

"You're sure?" Shelly whispered nervously.

"Yeah, I am." Jessie answered calmly. Much calmer than she felt.

She walks up to Jake and taking his hands pulls him to his feet and turns to the steps.

"Where are you taking me?" He teased.

"Come into my parlor said the spider to the fly." She said coyly.

"Well, now what?" Dan looked to Shelly with imploring eyes.

She fidgeted with her hair. "We could go upstairs too."

Taking her in his arms, "we don't have to yet, you know."

She kissed him softly, sighing, "It's okay," and led him upstairs.

Jake rolled onto his side and held her close. "I've wanted that for a long time." As he kissed her gently.

She lifted her eyes to meet his. "I felt like it was time. After all, I love you." She whispered adoringly.

"Me too." He kisses her ear.

Pecking his lips she asked, "want something to drink?"

"Yeah. That make me thirsty."

"Me. Too," as she gets up to dress. She turns to him to say, "I'll be…" and noticed him staring at he oddly. "What?" Puzzled by his look."

"You never had sex before?" He whispered hoarsely. "This was your first time?"

"No." She answered simply. "And yes, it is my first time."

"Come here." He ordered her softly.

She walked to him. "What?" She asked sweetly.

He sits up and takes her in his arms. He hugs her tight. So tight that she laughed.

"Hey, I'm still breakable."

He kissed her so gently. "I'm sorry, Jessie. I just never expected… but I'm glad you were!" Kissing her again.

She runs her fingers through his hair. "I saved it for the one I love."

He kissed her again. His expression needed no words.

"I'll be right back." As she pulled away from him.

He lay back and looked at the spot on the bed again. He wanted to jump up and down on the bed and pound his chest like Tarzan. But men just don't do thins like that. His heart swelled with intense love.

She came into the room. Holding out the glass. "Lemonade."

"That'll do fine." As he takes the glass he pointed to the blanket. "You'd better take care of that."

Her eyes followed his fingers. "Oh!" And she blushed.

He stands and dresses. "Come on. We'll wash it." As he gathers it up he touches her cheek. "I love you."

"For always?" She whispered.

"Forever and a day." He promised. Holding up his pinkie for her to link with his.

Still holding onto him she pulls him to the radio and puts in a CD of slow music. Turning to him she curtsied. "May I have this dance?"

He pulled her into is arms and slowly sways with her. As he spins her he nibbles on her ear.

Snuggling closer. "I'll give you all night to stop that."

Laughing into her eyes he starts spinning her.

"No, no." She laughs. "I meant the ear."

He picks her up and as he turns slowly with her he nibbles at her ear.

As chills run up and down her spine she giggles. "Jake put me down."

"Or what?" He challenged her.

She blushes as she says, "Oh, I'll just make love to you again." She whispered against his ear.

He carries her to the bed and laying her down, his eyes never leave hers. Slowly he lowers his lips to hers as he lay beside her. Chills run the length of her body as she gives herself in sweet abandonment.

"You're wonderful." She whispered sweetly.

"Aw, my love. So are you." Touching her lips gently with his fingers.

They get dressed, and taking the blanket, put it in the washer. "Do you want a sandwich?" As she walks to the fridge.

"Sure. What have you got?" peering over her shoulder.

"Let's see. How about ham and potato salad?"

"That's fine." He kissed her neck.

"You're giving me goose bumps." She laughs as she pulls away from him.

"Umm," he said softly.

"Jake," as she turns to face him, "you can't be thinking…"

"Who says?" He smiles wickedly at her.

"You are, aren't you?" She puts her arms around his neck. "You devil!"

"Only for you." He answered against her lips.

"And we're standing here with the fridge door open."

He turned her away and pushed it shut. "There, now it's closed."

"Well at least let me put this down." Holding out the food.

Taking it from her and placing it on the table he pushed her against the fridge.

"Jake," she pleads, "not right now."

"Why not?" Against her neck.

"Oh, I did awaken the devil in you!" She laughs.

"Mmm, yep, you did." He kisses her tenderly.

"Did you hear that?" She whispered as she looked past him.

"What?" He looked around to see what she was pointing at.

She pushed him away and ran from the kitchen. Squealing as he gave chase.

Catching her he pushes her onto the couch and falls on top of her.

"You're so bad," she said against his lips.

"You don't know the half of it." Smiling broadly at her.

Dan poked his head around the corner. "What's going on down here? It sounds like you are tearing the house down."

Jake, let's go of her and says, "sorry about that."

"Blame him," she points to Jake, "he started it."

"And I finished it." He laughs.

Dan looked at his watch. "It's two o'clock, man. Maybe we should be getting home."

"Is it really that late?" Shelly sighed. "Well. I hate to spoil the party, but I have to go."

"Looks like I'm outnumbered." Jake said clearly disappointed.

"Poor baby." Jessie teased.

He took her in his arms and kissed her. "I'll call as soon as We're done working on this car that's being picked up at noon."

"Okay," she smiled. "Shelly and I need to talk with you two and we all have to be serious."

"I'll call." He kissed her again.

Might," she called as he leaped from the porch.

She makes sure everything is locked and shut off, and goes to get ready for bed. She hesitates before laying down and bowing her head she prays, "Please don't let me dream tonight. Please.'

She sits up with a jerk. Looking around to see what it was that had awakened her. She is sitting on the couch and at the end of the coffee table is that form. With those large black eyes and that evil snarl. She sobs as it reaches for her. It grabbed her foot and pulled her onto the coffee table. She sees a knife in it's left hand as it spins her around on the table. She spins and spins, powerless to stop herself. It raises above her and the goo dropping from it's mouth falls on her face. As she stops spinning she sees the knife raised over chest. It hissed at her as it started to bring the knife down sharply to her chest. She screamed, "Nooo!" And it woke her up.

Sitting up and looking around, she realizes that she is still in her bed. She falls back and pressing her hands to her face sobs gently. She is covered with sweat, and trembling. She pushes the covers back and getting out of bed goes to the bath, and splashes cool water on her face. She looks at herself in the mirror and knows that something has to be done. She can't go on like this anymore. She goes downstairs and makes a cup of chocolate and sits at the table until she fells drowsy again. She found that climbing the stairs was a chore. She felt so drained this time. All she knew was that she wished something would happen so these dreams would stop. She is feeling certain now that Dave is just a pawn in the hands of another. She had this terrible feeling that it was Alice that represented the danger. Tonight was all to real! Sitting on the edge of her bed, not at all sure she wants to go back to sleep, she looks at the clock. Four-thirty. Still to early to get up. She sighs deeply and gets back into bed. She lay looking at the clock until her eyes droop. The last she remembers is singing the tune in her mind by Jim Reeves. "So sleep, sleep in peace and rest. Don't be afraid of the darkness. All's well, for over the land and the sea. God's keeping the night watch for you and for me."

****

III

The chirping of the Birds awakened her. She stretches as she opens her eyes. The sun was shining brightly, and as she stretches again, she sings with the birds. "Get up. Get up you sleepy head. Get up. Get up. Get out of bed." She stretches again and kicking the covers back gets out of bed. Getting dressed was a real chore this morning. Actually what she felt like doing was sleeping the day away. Hearing the phone ring she rushes down the stairs to answer it.

"Hello," she said sweetly.

"May I speak to Carol please?" She looked at her arms as she felt goose bumps raise on them.

"Who am I speaking to?" The woman on the other end sounded very perturbed.

"Her daughter, Jessica."

"I'll just call back later." She snapped.

"Can I tell her who called?"

"Alice. And I'll try back." She slammed down the phone.

Jessie pulled the phone back and stared at it for a moment. "How rude!" She replaced the phone and as she turned away it rang again.

"Hello."

"What are you doing?" Shelly asked her.

"Actually nothing. I was thinking about running to Burger King for Breakfast. Want to come?"

"Yes, 'cause I'm hungry. Pizza never seems to stick with me."

Jessie laughed, "When aren't you hungry?"

"Ha, ha." Shelly mocked sarcastically.

"I'll be right over to pick you up. Bye." She turns away and the phone rings again. "Hello," she says softly.

"Hi," Jake said. "I had to hear your voice this morning."

She chuckles. "Well I'm glad."

"This is really serious, Jessie."

"Do you mind?" She asked sweetly.

"No! And do you know why? Because I love you."

"I love you too." there was laughter in her voice.

"So I'll call you as soon as we're done here."

"Okay. I'll be waiting." She smiles to herself as she replaces the phone.

Shelly is waiting for her, and she bounds down the steps when she pulled up. As she gets in, she turns to Jessie.

"Wasn't last night wild?" She had a glow about her today.

"Ohhh, yeah!" She deepened her voice to give meaning to her words.

"So, did you do what you said you were going to?"

Smiling from ear to ear. "What do you think?" Waiving her brows.

"You did! You really did!" Shelly covers her mouth.

"Well! You knew I would someday." She looked sideways at her. "Didn't I always say that when the right man came along that I would seduce him?"

"You didn't?'" Shelly whispered. Her eyes large as a pool.

"Ohhhh, yes I did." She laughs. "Don't look so shocked. You know when I decide on something, I do it." Smiling. "Rather fitting huh? That I should be the one to initiate sex?"

"Well I did it too." Shelly replied smugly. "Only I didn't initiate it, Dan did."

"Are you okay with that?" Jessie asked her concerned.

"Yes actually. I am."

They never talked much about why she was nervous of having sex. It had been four years since the rape and they had never told a soul. This is the one thing that endeared them to one other. It had been awful. They were at a party that was supposed to be fun. And it was until some boys from across town at another school were invited and that's when the fun stopped. They were older that the others at the party and they had been drinking. One of them took a fancy to Shelly. He was nice looking and she was very young. He took advantage of her naiveness and she ended up being raped. Jessie still was red when she remembers how he held her down and had his way with her. She remembers just like it was yesterday, the way she had found them, and the way she had run at him and hit him several times before he sent her flying. She had gotten back up and cradled Shelly in her arms. Crying with her. She clearly remembers his snide remark. "How very touching." As he walked away.

"As long as you're sure." She sighed deeply. "I'd hate to see you hurt in any way after that bastard did what he did to you!"

She still got red necked when she thought about it.

"Really, Jess." Smiling sheepishly. "It was okay." She looked at Jessie for a long moment. "If you want the truth, I did want it. I did enjoy it, and I know that I'll do it again. Okay?" She sighs sadly. "He took my virginity, but he didn't take my life."

"He's still in there isn't he?"

"Last I heard he was. But then he hurt the next one pretty bad. She was even younger than me. I guess he got her to drinking, and then did his thing, and when she fought, he beat her up. What a prick! As sorry as I was for myself, I felt more so for her."

"How many girls ended up coming forward at the trial?"

"Seven," and she looked out the window. She often wondered why she hadn't been on of them. She knew that if she had been the only other one she probably would have, but as it turned out, there was more than enough. He'd be gone for a long, long time.

"You can bet there was probably a lot more that didn't come forward. They were as afraid of the publicity as you were. I wouldn't have been able to either." Gritting her teeth. "Bastard."

"Oh, Jessie. What am I going to do with you?" Shelly shakes her head and laughs.

Jessie just smiles as they whip into Burger King. "Are we going inside?"

"I'm not in any hurry. Are you?"

"None what so ever." Jessie says as she gets out. "I have to tell you about this dream I had after you guys left. Talk about freaky."

"Oh Jessie. I'm so sorry. I should have stayed with you."

"It wouldn't have mattered. I'd still dream."

"But you wouldn't have been alone."

"It's alright, Shelly." Smiling at her.

They go inside and Jessie looks around. "Let's sit back in that corner, so we can talk without a bunch of ears trying to hear what we say."

They get their food and take it to a spot away form the crowd.

"After you guys left. I went straight to bed. I lay there for a while thinking about Jake. He's so wonderful." She sighed.

"Boy, you've got it bad!" Shelly teased her.

"Shut up," Jessica shot back. "I'm trying to talk." She patted Shelly's hand and smiling says, "Anyhow, before I was rudely interrupted, I started to say that I dosed off and then it started. It was so real this time, Shelly, that I actually thought I was in my living room. I hear something and it wakes me up. I sit up, and I'm on the couch. And floating at the end of the coffee table is that form. Well it grabbed my foot and pulled me onto the table, and I started spinning. Around and around, real fast, and I could no nothing to stop it. It had a knife and as I slowed down, it hovered above me and raised the knife to stab me. That awful goo was dripping all over my face, and as it started to bring the knife down, I screamed, and woke myself up. I had to look around to make sure I was still in bed, that's how real it was."

"You couldn't get away from it?" Shelly looked concerned.

"I could do nothing. It was like this force had me and I was pinned down." She crumpled her paper in anger. "It's not fair that I should be having these stupid dreams."

"We really must do something."

"Oh, I quite agree! Something has to break, and I'm determined that it won't be me." As she remembered, "Oh, yeah. My mom's friend called me back last night. She said that I shouldn't do anything stupid, like try to get to know her. She said that she is best left alone. I guess she is real nasty, and doesn't like anyone. Donna said she had no friends, and please just stay away from her."

"If she works with her she should know, Jessie. Did you tell her about Dave?"

"Yes, but she doesn't know him. You know what, Shelly?" She leans in closer to her. "I'm not so sure that I think Dave is all that bad. He could be a pawn of sorts. You know, for that thing that wants to hurt me all the time.?"

"I think we really have to find out about this Alice. If we're careful and get the fellas to help. There is safety in numbers they say."

"Now let's change the subject. I want to know about last night." Jessie said smiling.

"You first." Shelly shook her head. "It was awesome! He was awesome!" She whispered excitedly.

"More. I want to hear more." Shelly ordered.

"Well," she clears her throat, "after we went up stairs... I pulled him onto the bed and lay on top of him. I was... a... totally the initiator." She said a little sheepishly.

"I still can't believe that," Shelly laughs at her.

"I'm afraid it's true. But I think he liked that I did that."

"And then what happened?" Shelly leans closer and looks into her eyes.

"We kissed this long, soft kiss, and then he rolls me over and touched my face ever so gently. I just melted. He kissed me again, and I said, do you want to make love. He asked me if I was sure." She laughs at that. "I was sure alright! So I slowly slid off the bed and started removing my clothes. It didn't take him long to do the same."

"Ohhh, you naughty girl!" Shelly squealed. "But this is totally delicious."

"He's totally delicious!" Jessie whispered delightfully. "But anyhow you can pretty well figure what went on after that. You should of seen the way he looked at me, Shelly." She threw back her head and laughed. "I loved it!"

"I enjoyed my experience too," Shelly offered shyly.

"I'm glad," Jessie said softly, "But you don't have to talk about it if you don't want to."

"I'm just not as brazen as you." She covered her mouth. "I'm sorry. I didn't mean it to come out like that."

"I know. And that's okay 'cause I have enough for the both of us." Jessie smiled broadly.

Shelly squeezed her hand. "You know I was only joking."

"But it's true isn't it?" Jessie answered nonchalantly.

"Dan's a wonderful guy too, Jessie. And he was so gentle last night. It was almost as if he knew that he needed to be." Her eyes twinkled. "It was wonderful."

"You know what, Shelly. I think our little differences is why we get along so well. I'm bold, and you're timid. Most of the time. I'm a go getter and you are content to follow. And yet we know that we can depend on one another through thick and thin. These little things make for a good chemistry, and that makes for a strong friendship." Tilting her head and staring into her eyes. "Don't you think so?"

Shaking her head, "I've often thought that."

"Ready?" Jessie stands to go.

As they walk to the car Shelly offers, "you know what? If this Alice person turns out to be this thing you keep dreaming about, she is probably mad. Any you know what they say about mad people. That they are super strong! We really have to be careful."

"I know." Jessie sighed. "I know."

They ride n silence. Both deep in though, wondering about her dreams.

"Do we have anything planned for today?" Shelly finally broke the silence.

"Maybe we should go to the beach. I'd like to see how the party went. To find out if we missed anything."

"Are you kidding?! We didn't miss a thing!" Shelly said exasperated.

Jessie laughed at her. "You are so gullible, Shelly. Of course we didn't miss anything. I wouldn't care if we missed out on winning a million bucks!" Glancing at her. "Last night will always be the most precious night of my life."

"Yeah," Shelly sighed.

"Do you want to come to my house? We can read some more n those books."

"Might as well. I don't have anything else to do." Looking at her for a moment, Shelly asks, "you don't really think that your mom is in any danger, do you?"

"I wish I knew. But just in case she is, we have to be aware of what she's doing at all times. We can't let her out of our sight. Of course, going to work isn't a problem. It's after that we have to worry about."

"What if she is invited to go from work to her house?"

"I would hope my mother would make some excuse as to why she couldn't except. She would suspect something. Or at least I hope she would. Remember, Donna told me she never invites anybody to her place. She's unfriendly and rude. Which reminds me. She called the house this morning wanting to speak to mother. Very unfriendly, and she was rude!"

"She called you house? See there, Jessie. Something isn't right here." Shelly is shaking her head.

"Two years she has worked at that office and never once did she call our house. Not once! This picture is getting grimmer by the minute. Don't you think?"

"Can't we go to the police?" Shelly ventured to ask.

"And tell them what? That we have strong suspicions that my mother is going to be hurt. They'd laugh us right out of City Hall."

"You're probably right."

"I feel so helpless. Like I know something is going to happen, and yet my hands are tied." She pulled into the drive and sits looking at Shelly for a moment, and then she says very sadly, "I know that if something happened to my mother I wouldn't want to go on living."

"Don't say that, Jessie." Shelly chided her.

"I can't help it, that's how I feel."

"I know, but let's not think that way." Touching her arm.

"Let's sit out on the porch," Jessie changes the subject. She goes in to get the books and then joined Shelly on the swing. She felt a heaviness to her heart that she couldn't explain, and hoped that she could find something by reading. Something that would give her an idea as to what was happening. All she knew was that she was more than ready to end the dreams that seemed to be coming more frequently now. They were both so deep into reading, that when the phone rings, they both jump.

"Gees on pete!" Jessie places her hand over her heart. "I've got myself so jumpy."

"And me too." Shelly laughs nervously.

"Hello," Jessie answered softly. "She points to the phone and mouths, "it's Jake. What am I doing? Sitting on the porch reading."

"Are we doing anything tonight?"

"Whatever you guys want is alright with us. Right, Shelly?" Who gives a thumbs up.

"Shelly's there huh? Dan was trying to call her."

"Ooops," as she glances at Shelly. "Dan was trying to get ahold of you."

"Sorry," she apologizes.

"Okay, we'll talk it over when we get there."

"Okay, but don't forget that we need to talk." Jessie implored him.

"We'll be there in an hour or so. And yes we'll talk. For now," he added meaningly.

"Alright," Jessie smiled a little sheepishly as she got the drift of his meaning. "Bye."

"Uh-oh. From the look on your face, someone is feeling amorous."

Jessie spread her hands. "What can I say?" As her cheeks turned a soft pink.

"What is this I see?" As Shelly touches a cheek.

Jessie pushes her hand away. "I told you he was wonderful." And with that she went back to reading and ignored Shelly's chuckling.

"I guess so," as she smiled wickedly.

"Let's change the subject before I get all hot and bothered." Jessie murmured. Burying her nose in the book signaling the end of the conversation. After a bit she cleared her throat and said, "This book says that a dream that turns into a reoccurring nightmare, usually pertains to an impending event. It could be a warning that you might have the power to change." She lays the book down. "I wonder…" She mused. "You know what we're going to do, Shelly?"

"I'm sure you're going to tell me." Shelly answered simply.

"When my mother and Dave gets here this afternoon, we'll have dinner ready to be served. And after a bit, I'll ask him about Alice. You watch his face to see if there is any reaction. I can't ask questions and watch his face too, but you can. Will you do that for me?"

"Do you think this is such a good idea?" Shelly was a bit nervous.

"Yeah. Yeah I do. And do you know what else? I'll have the boys here too. In case you get cold feet, I'll have them as backups."

"Gee thanks," Shelly replied a little sarcastic.

"No offense meant, Shelly, but it's better to be safe than sorry. Right?"

"But I wouldn't do that to you," Shelly pouted. "This means so much that I wouldn't dream of letting you down."

Taking her hands. "I know that. But we can still have the boys over." She leans back and sighs deeply. "Just think. We can fix them our first meal and work on solving a mystery at the same time."

"You're right. It just might work." Shelly is shaking her head.

"What? Jessie asked her laughing.

"It's you," Shelly laughs. "I see now why you chose the profession that you did. Personally I'd be afraid to dig into the minds of people. You just never know what they are going to do."

"But that's what intrigues me! Trying to understand how the mind works and what I can do to help. Do you realize that if you can help even one person, how rewarding it would be?"

Shelly studies her face. "I think you'll make a wonderful psychologist."

"I'm sure going to try."

"Not to mention the money you'll make." She laughs.

"I don't think that being an English major is anything to sneeze at."

"Jessie," as she reached for her hands, "Promise me we wont get like so many others. That after graduating we wont go separate ways."

Smiling at her, Jessie hugs her tightly. "We are not like so many others, Shelly. And I will never let us fade apart. Sisters forever!" And she holds up her right hand to lock with Shelly's.

"Forever," Shelly locks her hand and agrees willingly.

And they were like sisters. They had been close ever since kindergarten. Neither had another sibling, and their friendship had grown over the years to that of a sisterly feeling. Jessie was the stronger willed of the two, but also had a very tender heart. There was nothing one wouldn't do for the other.

"Now let's get serious about what to prepare for supper." She thinks for a moment. "I know, we'll go to the store and get a roast." She stands as she can feel the excitement starting to mount in her. "I'll get my purse." She grabs the books, and phone, and carries them inside.

"This is going to be fun." Shelly said as she too felt the excitement building.

"I think so too," as she backs out of the drive. "Let's see. I know I don't need to get potatoes or carrots, but I think I need celery. And what kind of bread do we want to serve?"

"How about Italian? And that's always good with any meal."

"Then we'll get a cherry pie and ice cream. That will make a nice solid meal. What do you think about that?"

"Mmmm, I'm hungry already." Shelly laughs.

They studied the roast, and finally settled on one that they both thought looked good. They hurry and do the shopping so they can beat the boys to the house.

"I hope Jake and Dan didn't come over already. We certainly don't want to get off on the wrong foot with them." Jessie said a little worried. As they pull up to the drive, they see Jakes car setting there.

"Busted!" Shelly laughed.

"Well, now what?" They both laughed at her nervousness. "Just go up to them and act natural. We'll explain about dinner, and hope they aren't mad."

"Hi," Jessie smiled as she stepped onto the porch. "Could you get the door for me, Jake?" She asked very sweetly.

He got up, and holding the door for her said, "We wondered what happened to you. I thought maybe you got cold feet." He added as he followed her to the kitchen.

She sets the bags on the table, and turning to him, takes ahold of his shirt. She pulls him close and kisses him. "Does that feel like cold feet?" She whispered into his ear.

Putting his arms around her, and smiling, "no, but you could persuade me a little more."

She kissed him again. A long sensuous kiss. "That will have to do for now, we have dinner to prepare."

"What's the occasion?"

"Okay. Let me get this in the oven, and then we'll sit down, and have that talk I mentioned. It all comes to this," as she points to the food she had purchased.

"What can I do to help," Shelly asked as her and Dan came in.

"Get the carrots out, and peel them. Put them into that pan." She points to a roaster sitting on the counter.

"Got ya."

Jessie handed the ice cream to Jake. "Could you put that in the fridge please?" She sets the pie on the counter. "I hope you guys like cherry pie."

"I do," Dan said quickly.

"Me too." Jake agreed.

"What's being celebrated?" Dan looked puzzled.

"We're fixing dinner for you." Shelly smiled at him.

"Wonderful!" Dan beamed, "but what's the occasion?"

"I'll tell you that after we get this into the oven." Jessie said.

Jessie peeled the potatoes, and sliced the celery, and arranged it around the meat. A little salt and pepper, and into the oven.

She turns to them and says, "It's time to talk." She takes Jakes hand and leads him into the living room. "Okay, it's like this. I told you about my dreams, but since then, there has been another. This one terrifies me to no end. It floats. It has this scummy grey skin, with these large black eyes that have a green florescent ring around them. It snarls, and hisses, and drips goo from it's mouth. It tried to stab me with a knife this morning. It seems so real." She paused to look at them. She definitely had their undivided attention. "Shelly and I talked with my mother, and found out that she was approached by a woman at work. Now that is the weird part. This woman has never liked my mother. Is never nice to her, doesn't talk to her. Actually she doesn't have anything to do with anyone at the office. Yet she wanted my mother to purchase insurance to protect me in case something happened to her. Everybody thought this odd. That she would show interest like that. Now comes the interesting part. In this book, it says that a reoccurring dream of this sort can be meant as a warning. That if you can figure out what it means, you have the ability to intervene. Shelly and I think this person, her name is Alice Watson, just might be the reason I've been having these dreams."

"What do you plan on doing?" Jake looks at her with concern.

"We thought that we would start to keep an eye on my mother. The only time we wont worry about her is when she is at work. Other than that, Shelly and I intend to follow her. I found out where this person lives too. I called a friend of mothers, her name id Donna. I told her about Dave, and all that's been happening, and she was very adamant that we should not try to get close to this woman. She is a very nasty person."

"We though that you two might be willing to help us. After all, you are two strong men," Shelly smiled sweetly at them. "And... There is safety in numbers."

"Boy," Jake sat forward and put his elbows on his knees. "Do you think we should really try to do this? If this person is that bad, she is best left to the police."

"And just what do we tell them, Jake?" Jessie asked, a little exasperated. "That I'm having these dreams. That we feel that they are a warning that something is going to happen to my mother." She stood up. "Believe me, I'd like nothing better than to go to the police, but I don't see that it's possible." She throws up her arms and starts pacing.

"Hey, calm down," Jake reaches for her, pulling her onto his lap. "You have a point there. And the way I see it is, we have no choice but to get involved. Because I have this feeling that you will do this yourself if we don't. Right?"

Jessie looks him square in the eyes. "Yes, Jake, I would. Only because I honestly believe my mother is in danger. Maybe even me."

He hugs her. "You win. I'm in. How about you, Dan?"

"Yes, I'm there. If she is that convinced of it, we have no choice but to get involved. Heck. I'm up to solving a mystery."

"I said you would be intrigued by a mystery." Shelly bragged.

Jake looks at both girls, and shakes his head. "Have you ever watched one of those programs about people that are insane? Seen how strong they are? I don't know if the four of us could even make a difference."

"But, Jake, we have to try!" She pleaded. "What if I'm right? What if this Alice person sent Dave to meet my mother, just to somehow get her interested in insurance? Then she would somehow get her name on there too, and then kill my mother?"

Everybody sat in dead silence.

"Okay. Now that I have you thinking, here's what we're doing tonight. We discussed this earlier. Shelly and I. We decided to cook dinner for mother and Dave. They'll be home this evening. We're going to ask you to stay also. After we've been sitting for a while, I'll bring up Alice, and the insurance, and you all watch Dave's face for any type of reaction. If he's a culprit too, we'll know. Is that okay?" She looks from Jake to Dan.

Jake spreads his hands. "Okay."

"I'm on your side," Dan smiled at Jessie.

She hugs Jake, and then jumps up, and goes over and hugs Dan. "Thank you both for believing in me." She sits back on Jake's lap, and lays her head on his shoulder. "Especially you."

He kisses her tenderly. "I can't have you getting hurt. As stubborn as you are, you'd try to take her on yourself. I can't allow that."

"Why don't we take a ride and see if we can find her house?" She asks brightly. She felt she had to do something to change the mood of everybody.

"Yeah, let's do that." Shelly said enthusiastically. "It's best to know ahead of time where she is at."

"We'll take my car because she wont know it." Jake offered. "And, Jessica, you keep a low profile. We don't her becoming suspicious of us."

"I promise," as she hugged him tight. "I know what I'll do. I have a straw hat upstairs, I'll wear that. Will that do? If you pull it down over my face, she wont see that it's me."

"Do you have something for me? Incase she has been watching, and knows me too?"

"Be right back." Jessica races up the stairs, with Jake right behind her.

He takes her in his arms and kisses her passionately.

"What was that for?" She asks very softly.

"For you spirit, and selflessness. Because I love you deeply. Or I could name a thousand other reasons for it." He kisses her again.

She touches his face ever so gently. "Jake, I do love you too."

He lifts her against his chest, and buries his face in her hair. "If anything happened to you…" He squeezed her.

"With you protecting me, Jake? I feel as if I could stand against the world and win." She smiled into his eyes. "Now we'd better go down before they come looking for us."

He laughs. "Let 'em look."

"No, really. We must do this." Jessie insisted.

"Later than?" Kissing her neck.

"Yes, later." She gives him a peck on the lips. "Now come on." And she pulls him down the steps.

"You're lucky you came down." Dan teased them. "I was about to come up after you."

Jake gives him a wicked smile. "You'd have seen some heavy petting."

Jessie blushed and said smartly, "stop it you two!"

They laughed at her.

Looking at them with a straight face, she says, "laugh it up fuzz ball."

Shelly lost it, and Jake, and Dan knew they'd been had.

"Here," Jessie hands Shelly a hat to put on. "Now let's go. Can we?"

"Alright. Alright." Jake said impatiently.

"Well. I want to get back here to check on dinner in an hour or so. What's wrong with that?"

Jake takes her by the hand, and leads her to the car. Opening the door for her, he kisses her as she sits down.

"Enough of that," Dan teased.

"What's the matter, Dan? Kissing make you nervous?" Jessie asks him very sweetly.

Dan looked at Shelly, and then back to Jessie. "Not really."

"You two have got to quit being so shy. If you're in love, show it." She turned and smiled sweetly at them. "A little public display is not unhealthy, you know." She gets up on her knees, and throws her arms out, and looking to the heavens shouts, "I'm in love, I'm in love, I'm in love!"

Dan looks at Shelly, and laughing says, "you're friend is nuts."

"She just loves life." Shelly defended her.

Jessie leans over and kisses Jake. "You see. I do love you."

"If I had any doubts before, I certainly don't now." He laughs as he takes her hand, and squeezes it. She kissed him again.

"Get a motel room!" Shelly teased.

"There you go!" Jessie agreed readily.

They all laugh at her, and Dan says, "Jessie, you're a real trip."

"I know," she answered smugly.

When they arrive at the lake, Jessie said, "Donna said that Alice lived at the far end of the lake." She points to the left. "Since that way is mostly beach, and boat docks, she must live out this way." And she points to the right.

"Remember to keep yourself sitting, Jessie. We don't want to draw any attention to ourselves if she out." Jake warned her.

"Oh, don't worry. I'm not going to mess this up."

The drive ran a couple of miles along the lake, and the houses were one after another. Jessie was beginning to think this may not be the lake Alice lived on after all.

"I think this road ends about another half mile or so." Jake looked at her. "Could she have meant somewhere else?"

Jessie raised her shoulders. "Donna just said out by the lake. I assumed that she met this one."

"There is still a few houses yet." Shelly offered. "Maybe it's one of those."

As they get near the end of the road, they see sitting back in amongst that trees, a small cottage style home. As they pass the mailbox at the end of the lane leading up to it, Dan looks at the box.

"Alice Watson. That's the place." Dan said a little excited.

"Is it safe for me to look?" Jessie asked from under her hat.

Dan looks around nonchalantly. "I don't see anything moving about up there."

Jessie takes a look at the house. "She lives comfortably I'd say. It is pretty out here, but it's a shame it's wasted on the likes of her." She spat.

Jake goes on down to the end, and turns around. As he starts back, he sees a car coming at them. "Uh-oh. Keep you're head low girls. This could be her."

"I wish I could remember what she looks like." Peeking out from under her hat.

Jake glances over at her as he passes her car. The woman driving looked straight ahead as if she didn't even notice them. "So what do you think? Was that her?"

"I think so, but I only saw her once, and that was a while ago." She sighed in exasperation. "Darn it. I just wanted to know for sure."

Looking into his side mirror. "She stopped at the mail box. I'd say it's her." Jake said.

"Well, now that we know where she lives, we can keep an eye on her." Jessie looked around, and watched her go up the drive.

"And just how are you going to do that?" Jake demanded. "There's no place to hide, and since that's the last house on the road, you can't pretend to be going anywhere else."

She sighed a very heavy sigh. "I'll think of something."

"Jessica!" He threatened. "If I have to, I'll hog tie you!" He looks firmly at her. "Understand?"

She remained quiet, and looking straight ahead said nothing.

"Didn't your friend tell you not to go trying to get too close to her? That she is best left alone?" Barely holding his temper.

"Yes, she did." She answered simply.

"Then you'd better damn well listen." He's angry now.

"Take a chill pill." She tries to laugh it off.

"He's right, Jessie. If you're going to try anything other than what we planned, then count me out." Shelly said firmly.

"Likewise,' Dan agreed just as firmly.

"Party pooper!" Jessie glanced sideways at Shelly.

"Call me what you like. I mean it." Shelly shot back.

She glanced from one to the other, and knew they were serious about what they said. "Well, at least we know where she lives now. If mother should happen to not come home, and we can't find her, then we'll know where to look. Right?"

"Just as long as you're not going to be stupid." Jake replied without looking at her.

"I'm not." Jessie answered meekly.

"Now that we have that settled, where to?"

"Back to the house. We girls have to check on dinner." Jessie reaches for Jakes hand. He stares into her eyes without saying a word, and then back to the road.

The ride back was mostly silent, and Jessie knew that she had gone too far this time. She now had the task of convincing him that she wouldn't do anything without him. Without any of them.

As she opened the door to the house, they all breathe in deeply. "When are we eating?" They all chimed.

Smiling, "around five or six. If mother and Dave aren't here by then, well, we'll eat without them."

Jake moaned as he hugged her. "That's at least another hour and a half."

"Just think how much you will enjoy it when we get to sit down and eat." Smiling up at him.

"Let's sit out on the porch." Shelly takes Dan's hand.

"I have to check the roast first." Jessica pulled it from the oven. Jake and Dan peering over her shoulder. Lifting the lid, she smiled as they took a deep whiff.

"Can't we eat now?" Dan pleads with her.

Shelly laughs at him, and taking his hand, pulls him, "Come on. Let's go out. Away from temptation."

Dan strains mockingly towards the food as she pulls him. "Heaven. I'm in heaven."

Jessie puts the lid back on the pan, and closes the oven door. "Out," as she shows them toward the door.

Jake walks backward, sniffing the air. "At least get us a pop."

"Okay. You help me." As she hands him a couple of cans.

"Do you want to go to the beach later?" Jake asks as he pulls he onto his lap.

"Sure," she sighed. "I think I need to relax."

"I think you do too, Jessie. You're scaring me." Shelly agreed.

"She scaring all of us!" Jake and Dan echoed together.

"I'm sorry, guys. Really I am." She looks at them. "Sometimes I forget that not everybody is not like me. Or thinks like me." She sighs. "And I know that acting on what I feel isn't always the best thing to do. And I promise you all that I wont do anything that we haven't discussed amongst us."

Jake hugs her. "You don't know how much better that makes me feel."

Laying her head on his shoulder. "I think I do."

"So Jake, tell us again what we're doing at supper. This might be the only chance we get at questioning Dave."

"Okay." She sits up. "After we've been eating for a bit, I'll ask Dave how long he's known Alice. While I'm talking to him, you all watch him close for any sign of discomfort at the mention of her name. If he does something, one of you is bound to catch it."

"We can handle that." Shelly said. "What if we do get a reaction, Jessie? What then?" "I don't know," She answered sadly. "Because it's my mother who is going to get hurt here."

Jake hugs her. "Let's not jump to any conclusions yet. Wait 'til we talk to him first. You never know. He might not be dishonest."

"I feel the same way," Jessie agreed with him. "I think the one we have to worry about is Alice. Somehow, she intended on getting her hands on mothers papers, and putting her name on there as beneficiary. I'm sure of it."

"But why?" Shelly looked puzzled.

"Let's hope we find out before it gets that far!" Jake replied.

"Amen!" Dan said enthusiastically. "What if this person is from your mothers past?"

"Hum… I wonder?" Jessie mused.

"But surely your mom would remember her? Especially if she's as nasty as everyone says she is." Shelly said.

"There has to be a logical explanation for all of this. And I feel that somehow, we'll be finding out real soon what it is." Jessie started.

"So we're all agreed that no matter what, we don't, none of us," looking at Jessie with meaning, "do anything without us all being there?" Jake demanded.

"Here," Dan said raising his hand.

"Me too," Shelly agreed.

"You have my complete promise," Jessie said seriously.

"Thank you." Jake pulls her close, and hugs her.

"I'm sorry I acted the way I did." Smiling sheepishly.

"Do we forgive her? We the jury." Jake asked the others.

"Well, she did cause us some serious stuff back there." Dan said as he looked at Shelly. "What do you think?"

Frowning at her, Shelly said, "she did promise. And I know for a fact that when Jessie promises something, you can believe it." She paused. "Okay. Let's forgive her."

"But don't do it again!" Jake said firmly. "Or else!"

"Oooh, that sounds very threatening." Jessie pretends to cower.

"I hope so," Jake shakes her.

They all look up as a car pulls up to the curb.

"Okay everybody. Here's where our plan starts." Jessie breathed.

Dave gets out, and comes around to open the door for Carol. Taking her bag, he walks her to the porch.

"Well, look at you two. All nice and sun burnt." Jessie laughs.

"It was worth it," Dave said as he came onto the porch.

"What's that smell?" Her mom sniffs the air. "You cooked dinner." She looked at Jessie in amazement.

"Shelly and I did." As she hugs her mom.

"You timed that perfectly. How did you know what time we would be home?" Dave asked, perplexed.

"A lucky guess. You will stay won't you." She asked very sweetly.

"With it smelling that good! You bet!"

They all laugh, and she grabs Shelly's hand. "Come on, Shelly. Let's set the table."

"Me too," Jake offered to help.

"Don't leave me out," Dan followed them.

Everybody laughs again.

This just might turn out to be alright, Jessie thinks, as they enter the kitchen. "Plates up there, and glasses there." Jessie said to the boys. "How about wine? Do we want some?"

"Fine by me," Jake agreed.

"Mother? Do you want wine?"

"Sure," Dave answered as he came to the doorway. "Can I do anything to help?"

"No. There's enough of us out here getting in the way." She laughs at him.

Opening the oven door, as Jake, and Dan carried dishes past her, to the dining room. She takes a deep breath, and savors the aroma. She didn't realize how hungry she was until now. Shelly grabbed the silver wear, and napkins, and smiled at her as she walked by.

"You know what, Dave? You can do something. Get the wine from the fridge, and pour it for us." Giving him a sweet smile.

"I can handle that."

Shelly comes back into the kitchen, and gets a bowl for the vegetables. "That looks delicious, Jessie." She looks up to make sure Dave isn't near. "I think they're both smitten."

"Who's bitten?" Carol asks as she comes into the kitchen.

"Hand me that plate, will you?" Jessie looked at Shelly. "I might need help getting this out. It's cooked really tender."

"That's the way you want it," her mom said smiling. "Do you want me to get it out for you?"

"Maybe you'd better. You're the pro." She stepped back and let her mom take over. Her and Shelly looked at one another, and she motioned across her brow and mouth, "Whew!" Shelly shook her head in agreement.

"Look, mom. We even got cherry pie, and ice cream."

"This is wonderful, girls. I was just going to improvise for us."

"Well, now you don't have to." Jessie said proudly. "Oh, you know what?" Putting her hand to her mouth. "I forgot to make coffee."

"Go ahead and do it. It'll be done in a couple of minutes." Her mom said as she carried the meat to the dining table. "Dig in," as she sat it down.

"We've been waiting a couple of hours for this," Jake said. "You don't have to tell me twice."

They laughed as he filled his plate.

"Mmmmm," Jake said as he took a bite. "You girls out did yourselves here."

"This is great!" Dan said in agreement.

"Thank you," They say together.

"Well I must certainly say that I agree." Dave looked at them. "This is heavenly."

They both blush at this praise. "Thanks."

Carol just smiled, and took a bite of meat.

"Who wants coffee?" Jessie asked as she got up to get it.

"Dave and I will have a cup." Her mother smiled.

"I'll wait until desert," Jake said, as he took another bite.

"Same here," Dan agreed.

"We have dessert too?" Dave raised his brows. "These girls know how to entertain." He smiled at Carol.

As Jessie sets their coffee down, "so you had a good time did you?"

"A very good time." Carol answered, smiling into Dave's eyes.

"We had a great time! Everyone liked you're mom." Dave looked at Jessie smiling.

"That's understandable." Jake offered quickly.

"I bet you're glad Alice introduced you two." Jessie said coyly.

"That's the only good thing she's done for me." Dave frowned.

"That bad, huh?" Jake asked nonchalantly.

"He's seen the side the rest of us has, and then a bit more." Carol smiled at him.

"They know of her then?" Dave asks. "Well, some," she sighed. "I don't talk much about her."

"So how long have you known her?" Jessie asked casually.

"Let's see… Seven months." He counting in his head. "Yeah, about that." He sighed. "I try to forget when it comes to her."

"What was her reason for introducing you two?" Jake asked curiously.

"She does have extra insurance with me. They really don't have enough at the office. Then she told me about this woman who had lost her husband a couple of years ago, and had a young daughter. She offered to set us up so I could sell her some coverage." He looked at Carol. "Hence, I met Carol, and the rest is history."

"Is she really as nasty as I hear?" Jessie made a face.

Dave laughs. "Believe me, she's nasty!" Taking Carols hand. "To give you an idea. When she found out I was dating you. She flipped off the deep end. Wanted to know what was wrong with her, that I chose you instead? She slapped me, and told me to get out of her house." He touched his face. "I can still feel it. She packed quite a wallop!"

"Really?" Jessie asked, surprised. "She strong huh?"

"You could say that," he replied laughing, and touching his face.

Jessie looked at her mother. "She called here this morning."

Carol frowned. "For what?"

"She wanted you, and she was quite rude to me."

"I'll have to say something to her about that." Carol said in anger.

"Please don't do anything to make her angry, mother. I don't care that she was rude to me." Jessie pleaded with her.

"I think she's right, Carol. She probably tried to get ahold of me, and when she couldn't find me, called to see if you were home." He sighed. "I guarantee you that when I get home, there will be umpteen calls from her on my machine." Sighing deeply, he takes her hands. "I want you to be careful."

"Gee, guys," Jessie implored. "I didn't want to ruin dinner this way."

"You know what? It's probably a good thing you did." Dave smiled at her, "Other wise I would have walked in unexpecting, and got bombarded."

They laugh at that. "Maybe some good came of it after all." Her mother answered.

More than you know, Jessie thought. "Does anyone want more wine? Shelly, would you get the coffee pot?"

"I'll have another glass," Dave held up his glass.

"Mother?" She held the bottle up.

"Yes. Half a glass. Then that'll do me."

"Are we finished eating?" Jessie smiled at the boys, as she picked up the plate.

"Here, I'll help you," Jake offered as he got up from the table.

"Who all wants coffee?" Shelly asked as she held out the pot.

"You can pour me some now," Dan answered.

"Yeah, me too." Jake said as he takes he, and Dan's plates to the kitchen.

"What do you think?" Jessie whispered as they sat the plates on the counter.

"He's a cool dude. There was absolutely nothing but anger when you asked about Alice."

She hugged him tight. "You don't know how happy you just made me."

"Yes I do. It's all over your face." He touched her cheeks.

"Mother really likes him."

"That's readable too." As they walked back into the room.

"Are you finished, mother?"

"You can have my plate. That was very good girls. Thank you."

"Very good!" Dave handed her his plate.

"Dessert everybody?" Jessie asked. "Shelly, will you help me?"

"Did you see anything?" She whispered as they walked back to the kitchen.

"The only thing I got, was that he didn't care much for Alice. Honest opinion? I don't think he's up to anything. I think he's as smitten with your mother, as she is with him!"

Jessie laughs as she replies, "that's very obvious isn't it? Didn't I tell you he was good looking?"

"And likeable." Shelly smiled fondly. "I certainly can't picture him in a dress. Not even for a moment!"

They both laugh at that thought.

"Mmmm. Look at this," As she put a piece of pie on a plate.

Shelly followed with ice cream. "Let's hurry. My mouth is watering."

"Soups on." As she sets down the tray. "Mother. Dave." She looks at him, "I hope you like cherry pie."

"Yes, ma'am, I do." Taking it from her hands.

She hands a piece to Jake, and Dan.

"Gee, Jessie," Dan laughs at her, "Do you think you're feeding a horse?" Looking at the size of his pie.

"You're growing boys." She smiled sweetly.

"Evidently." Jake laughed.

After they finished dessert, Jessie looked at them as she cleared the table. "And you boys are helping with the dishes."

"I am not." Jake stated frankly.

"Yes you are," smiling sweetly at him. "Besides, silly, we have a dishwasher. Just spray them off, and in they go."

"Oh, alright," Jake grumbled.

"There, mother. You and Dave can sit on the porch and relax." Jessie smiled at them. "We'll have things done in no time." She takes Jakes hand, and leads him to the kitchen. "You don't have to help me, Jake. That was just an excuse to let those two be alone."

"Dan and Shelly followed them to the kitchen carrying dishes.

"I'll help, Jessie." Shelly sat the dishes down.

Jessie looks at the guys, her eyes dancing mischievously. "You two can stand there and look pretty."

"I don't look pretty!" Jake grabs her and pulls her close. A plat with some cherry juice was sitting by him. He put his fingers into it, and wiped it down her face.

"Jake!" She tried to pull away. "Stop it this instant!" Ignoring her, he rubbed it in.

"Tell me to look pretty." He scoffed at her.

"Okay, I'm sorry." She laughing now as she looks at Shelly, "It's a man thing."

"And don't you forget it!" She starts to kiss her, but pulls back. "I'm not kissing you until you wipe your face off."

"You put it there." She hands him a paper towel. Her tone said, you wipe it off.

"What am I supposed to do with this?" He holds it up, and looks at it as if he had no idea what she wanted.

"Oh, give me that," as she snatches it from him. "I'll do it myself."

Jake is laughing at her now.

She gives him a look, and starts to say something, but he cuts her off.

"I know. You're going to say; laugh it up fuzz ball." He twisted his face up, and mimicked her. He looked ridiculous.

The others lost it. Tears running, and laughing, Jessie tries to say, "enough already." She wipes her face, takes a deep breath, and in a crackling voice says, "Shelly, let's do the dishes." "Okay," Shelly answered wiping her face too. She turned to Dan, and still chuckling said, "just sit down, or go out on the porch and talk to Dave."

"Yeah, do that." Jessie said smiling. "We won't be but a few minutes."

"That's probably a good idea," Dan agreed.

"I know it is!" Jake smarted off.

Jessie touches his arm. "My face is clean now." She was hinting he could kiss her now.

Pretending to be scrutinizing her face, "so it is," but made no move to kiss her.

"What?" She pouted. "No kiss?" Looking hurt, and sticking out her bottom lip.

He looked at her for a moment. "No wait. Here's a spot." And he licks it. "And another," as he slowly moves his tongue down her cheek, to her lips. Pulling her tight, he kisses her soundly. "Is that what you wanted?" He asked in a husky voice.

She blushes. "Well…" She hesitated.

"I don't believe it. Jessie is at a loss for words." Dan said in amazement.

Shelly pushes him from the kitchen. "Go," she said jokingly.

Jake reluctantly releases Jessie, and follows him.

Jessie hugs her, "he does love me! Oh, Shelly, that was awesome! Just awesome!"

"It looked awesome." Shelly smiled brightly. "I guess you are lucky in every sense of the word."

"See why I say a little public display doesn't hurt?" Smiling at Shelly. "Sometimes good things can come from it." She takes Shelly's hands. "You have to quit being so shy. There's a lot of love for you out there," pointing to the porch.

Shelly sighed. "I know, Jessie. And I'm trying, but I still have a little trouble."

"I know you are. But try to remember that Dan is a totally different person." She whispered softly to her. "You just might a whole new way of feeling."

"I know, I need to open up more." Shelly whispered back.

"I'll give you a little help if you would like."

"How?" Shelly looked at her oddly.

"You just watch me when we're all together. I'll give you these looks, or motion with my head. Things like that. Okay?"

Shelly smiles, and says a little excited, "Okay!"

"I'll make you just like me." Jessie said proudly.

"Just like you?" Shelly raised a brow. "Maybe half like you."

Jessie laughed at her. "Could you imagine two of me?"

"No," Shelly answered truthfully. "Now let's get these dishes done before the boys come in to see if we fell in."

They laugh at that remark, and dive into doing them up.

"There," Jessie said as she wiped off the table. "We're done."

"And not a minute too soon," as she points a thumb at the door.

"I thought we'd come and see if you two needed help." Jake looks at his watch. "You said a few minutes."

"Sorry, but we had a little discussion to take care of. You know," she wrinkled her nose, "girl stuff?"

"Aww," was Jake's only reply.

"How about we go for a ride? That way we can talk freely about you know what." Jessie reaches for Jake's hand.

"I was going to see if you wanted to go sit at the beach, or in the park?" Jake said as he put his arms about her.

Jessie and Shelly's eyes meet, and she motions with her head for her to make a move.

Shelly slowly walks over and puts her arms around Dan, smiling into his eyes. "Did you enjoy your meal?" She asked sweetly.

He pulled her close and kissed her tenderly. "Yes, ma'am, I did."

She looks into his eyes, and blushes.

"Okay, people. Are we going or what?" Jake questioned.

"Or what," Shelly offered slyly.

Dan asked quietly. "Do you want to go somewhere alone?"

"You can't," Jessie said. "Not right now, that is. We really need to talk, and it's only seven-thirty." Smiling at Jake, "we have the rest of the night."

"Ready everybody? Let's get this over with, so we can enjoy ourselves." He looks at Jessie with meaning. She blushed.

As they come out to the porch, Jessie says to her mother, "We're going for a ride, mom."

"Alright, dear." She looked at Jake, and smiling said, "Drive carefully."

"Yes, ma'am." He offered his hand to Dave. "It was nice meeting you, man."

Dave stood, and shook his hand. "Likewise. Hey, Carol was telling me your dad has his own garage. He has some pretty old cars in there I bet."

"Yes he does. Why don't you stop over sometime and look around. We own some nice cars. And some of the ones we get to work on make your mouth water, so to speak."

"Yes, I'll have to do that."

Dan shakes his hand. "It was good to meet you, sir."

"Sir? Now I haven't had a young fella call me that for some time now." He smiled.

"I told you they were nice boys." Carol smiled sweetly at them.

Jessie hugged Jake. "That's my guy."

"Are we ready?" Jake asked to get out of an embarrassing moment.

"Let's go," they all say together.

"Bye," Jessie waves as they pull away, and Jake beeps.

"I'll tell you what, Jessie. I like that fella." Dan said honestly.

"I know. He's really nice." She sighed. "So that puts us back to square one."

"He knows Alice. He sells insurance. I think he had nothing on his mind but that. To make a sale. But after he met your mom, he couldn't help but like her. She's such a sweet person." Dan said.

"Isn't she though?" Shelly agreed with him. "I can't believe she hasn't had a boyfriend before this."

"She never met anybody that clicked like this one did." Jessie laughs as she says, "believe me when I say there's been a lot of calls."

They rode in silence for a while, then Shelly asked, "where are we going?"

"I thought we'd show you this spot we found a while back. I was riding around and saw this lane. I followed it, and it took me to a very secluded place."

"I hope you were alone," Jessie said with meaning.

"Nope. Dan was with me."

"How come you didn't ask us?" Jessie pouted.

"We were trying out an engine we had put into that Mercury dad bought. You have to put a few miles on to make sure there are no kinks." He looked at her mischievously. "Don't worry. There were no girls with us."

"Oh," she smiled sheepishly, because he had read her mind.

"It's a good thing. Otherwise, I might have to pull her hair out." Shelly answered jokingly.

Dan pulled her close, as he laughs, staring into her eyes. "Don't even think that way, babe. You're the only girl for me."

She lifted her lips to kiss his, and kissed him gently. "I'm glad to hear that."

"Yeah, me too." Jessie said in relief.

"Here we are," as he turns into a narrow lane. "It looks as if someone was going to build up here at one time, but changed their mind."

"I wonder why?" Jessie looks around, and was instantly struck with it's beauty.

"There could be a hundred reasons why." Jake answered her.

"I hope it wasn't because they broke up. Or that one of them died." Jessie said sadly.

"I have an idea." Dan said, a little excited. "Why don't we camp out here some night, and see if there are any ghosts.

Jessie turned to him, her eyes suddenly bright. "Do you mean that? I've always wanted to do things like that, but everyone else is either chicken, or just not interested."

"Sure, I'm serious," Dan answered her. "Maybe there was a pair of lovers going to build their dream house here. Sometimes, when two people are so bound by love, that even in death, they don't let go."

Jake looked at Dan. "I didn't know you were into this kind of stuff." He parked the car, and turned to look at him.

"Just never mentioned it. Actually, when I go to college, it will be to study the paranormal. I'd like to get into Ghost hunting eventually."

"Maybe I'll change my major then," Shelly said quickly. "I can't have you chasing around the country without me."

"It's something to think about." Dan said as they climbed out of the car.

"Can't you take a course on that too, Shelly? Then just continue with your English major?" Jessie asked a little worried.

"Yep, that's right." Jake spoke up. "Dan and I will one day be partners in my dad's shop. He'll have that as his major."

"Makes sense," Shelly agreed.

"Wow! It's beautiful up here." Jessie reached for Jakes hand as they strolled through the trees.

Dan put his arm around Shelly. "There must be hundreds of acres out here." Shelly said in awe. "You know, Jess. This would be the perfect spot to build our homes one day."

"That's part of the reason we came up here tonight." Jake put his arms around Jessie, and pulled her close. "To see what you thought of it."

Jessie looked at him funny. "Why would you want to do that?" She whispered.

He stopped walking, and looked into her eyes. "Because I want to make you my wife." He kissed her. "And dad said he'd help me out. I don't know, Jess, it's like it was meant to be."

"Are you asking me to be your wife, Jake?" Jessie whispered in shock.

He kneels at her feet, and reaching into his pocket, pulls out a ring. "Will you marry me Jessica." As he takes her finger, and puts the ring on it.

She falls to her knees, and hugs him tightly. "Yes. Oh yes!" And she kissed him boldly.

Dan had led Shelly away from the other, and taking her into his arms, asks her, "Shelly? Do you love me enough to be my wife?"

"Of course I do, silly. And I'll try to show it more." Smiling at him.

He reached into his pocked, and taking her left hand, "Shelly, will you marry me?" He puts the ring on her finger.

"I would have married you two years ago, Dan." And she kissed him.

"You would have?" Dan asked dumbfounded.

I've been in love with you since ninth grade." She said simply.

"And I didn't even know." He shook his head.

"Guys are like that," she kissed him tenderly. "But I held onto my dreams. I hope that one day, you would realize that you loved me too."

He kissed her lovingly. "I do now."

"Where are you two at?" They heard Jake holler for them.

Shelly put her hand over Dan's mouth as he went to reply. "Shhh."

"Got ya," he whispered as they hid behind a big tree.

"Hey? Where are you?" Jake hollers again.

"I saw them head this way." Jessie pulls Jake's hand.

As they come to the tree where they were hid, Dan jumps out, "got ya!" As he grabs Jessie's arm.

She screams and jumps. They laugh at her.

"Maybe we found Jessie's weak spot," Dan teases her.

"If you'd been having the dreams I've been having lately, you'd be jumpy too." She defended herself.

"Chill pill, Jess. I'm only joking." Dan replied.

"So what do you think? Is this place awesome or what, Jessie?" Shelly asked in excitement.

"it's simply beautiful. I could be content here." she sighs as she looks around.

"Come on, we have something for you." Jake pulls Jessie with him. He opens the trunk, and hands Dan a couple of blankets. Setting a small cooler on the ground and handing Jessie some cups.

"That tree looks like a good spot," Dan points at a large tree.

"Lead the way," Jake said as he followed.

They spread the blankets, and pull the girls down beside them. Jake opened the cooler and took out a bottle of champagne.

"What's that for?" Shelly asked.

"to celebrate our engagements." Jake answered. "You two had this planned?" Shelly looked into Dan's eyes.

He smiled. "It was Jake's idea."

"You buggers!" Jessie hugged him. "No wonder I love you!"

She kissed him.

Laughing at her, "I love you too." He poured the champagne, and held up his cup. "A toast." Looking at Jessie adoringly. "May we always be in love, and have happiness. And most important of all," looking at the others, "is that we all stay as close as we are at this moment in time."

They touch their cups together, and say in unison, "Amen!" They tipped their cups, and downed the drinks.

Jessie and Shelly coughed and sputtered. "Ugh! that's awful."

The boys laughed at them as Jake poured another round.

"To love and friendship." Holding up their cups.

"Here. Here," Dan said.

After they finished the bottle, they lay in one another's arms, and chatted idly. The boys were totally relaxed, the girls were giggly.

"I drank too much," Jessie said as she pressed her hands to her face. "Why'd you let me do that, Jake?"

"It was a celebration. We'll just stay here for a while, and then go somewhere and have a cup of coffee." He rolled onto his side. "There's some Pepsi in there, if you think it will help."

"Yeah, I'll try one." She sits up too fast, and falls right back again. "Whoa!," she laughed at herself.

"Maybe we should have only let one them have a few cups." Dan said. He was having a hard time not laughing at them.

Jessie tried sitting up again. This time she moved slower. She didn't want that felling of falling again. Even though it wasn't all that far to the ground, it felt like it was.

"Here," Jake handed her the Pepsi. "And don't guzzle it. It just might make you sick."

She stares at him with big eyes, and starts laughing.

He looks at Shelly. "Do you want one?"

"Yes please," as she sits up slowly. Her eyes meet Jessie's, and she starts laughing too.

Taking a deep breath, Jessie tried to gain some composure. Then looking at Jake, she asked, "Are we allowed to talk about Alice?" That's why we went for a ride. To discuss a plan."

"That's hat you thought we went for a ride for." He answered her. "But, Dan and I had other plans. Making your plans can wait until tomorrow."

"Sneaky. That's what I call it." She laughed.

"But didn't you love it, Jessica?" He touched her cheek gently.

"Yes, it was beautiful." She leaned over to kiss him, and lost her balance.

Jake caught her, and sitting her pop on the grass, he gently pushed her down, and leaned over her. "You're beautiful," he kissed her tenderly. "You are my life, Jessica. I was afraid you'd find somebody else while off at school."

"Never!" She breathed vehemently.

"I'm glad to hear that." He touched her gently. Running his fingers over her lips, "did you know that your lips are perfect?" He kisses them. "And that your neck is enticing?" He kisses it too. "And your breasts are lovely?" He kisses her there also.

"Jake," she whispered. "Stop it." She giggled.

"Why?" He asked against her lips.

"Because, silly, we aren't alone." She giggled again.

Jake looks at the other two, and says, "you know what? I don't really think that they are noticing anything." As he pointed his thumb toward them.

Jessie raised her head, and instantly laid it back down. Her hands to her forehead. "That's wonderful," she whispered. Smiling a beautiful smile.

"It is? Why do you say that?" He looks at her oddly.

"Oh, that's something I'll never tell!" She shakes her head no. Immediately regretting it.

"Never? Why?" He thought he was getting tricky.

Shaking her finger at him. "Oh no you don't! I might be tipsy, but I still know what's being said." She laughs at him. "No no no." And she starts giggling.

"Do you still want to leave?" He kissed her neck. He kissed her eye lids. "Do you?"

She pulls his head down, and kisses him. "We could move to a more secluded spot," she answered against his lips.

He gets up without another word, and helps her up. Grabbing the blanket, and taking her hand, he starts to lead her to a large tree several feet away. She's giggling at him, and losing her balance, falls. She is giggling uncontrollably, and he is laughing at her, and in trying to help her up, he falls too.

"I'm sorry," Jessie said between giggles. "Just give me a minute. My head is spinning." She giggles again.

"Well, open your eyes." He's trying to regain his composure. "Being tipsy does that to you. Open your eyes and I'll help you up."

Opening her eyes, she giggles, "are you sure?"

"Yes I'm sure. Now come on." And he heaves her up on her feet. He puts his arm around her to keep her from falling again.

"Okay. Okay. I'm going to get a grip here. Just let me take a few deep breaths." She stands to her full height. "There. Now I'm ready." She takes a step, and promptly fell on her butt. She leans forward, and laughs uncontrollably.

Jake sits down by her. "You're funny," he says laughing at her. "I guess I should have never let you drink that much. You've never had champagne before?"

"No, Jake, I haven't." She tried awfully hard to keep a straight face.

He gets up. "Let's try this again." Taking her hands, he pulls her up slowly, and puts his arm around her. He pulls her close, and leads her so she doesn't fall again. When they reach the tree, he gently lets go of her, and spreads the blanket. And taking her hands, sits her down slowly.

"See. We made it." She giggled.

Jake laughs, "so we did." He pushes her back. "Now where were we."

"You were kissing my breasts." She giggled.

He leans over her, and kisses her lips. "Do you want to get naked?"

She kisses him fervently. "Yes, let's get naked." She whispers.

He helps her undress, then removes his own clothes. Laying down, he takes her in his arms. "Are you ready for the devil you awakened in me?" He asks mischievously.

"Umm," She says against his lips.

Across the way, Dan is having problems of his own with Shelly. "Will you quit giggling? I can't help you if you don't help me too." As he tries to get her shorts off.

"I'm sorry, Dan. I drank too much." She's trying to be serious.

"No shit!" He's laughing as he finally pulls them off.

As he lay beside her, she whispered, "I'm sorry. I really am."

"Don't worry about it." He touches her face gently. "I shouldn't have let you drink so much." And he kisses her softly.

"But it was a special occasion. Besides, I had fun." She giggled.

"Yeah," he laughed at her. Looking into her eyes, "do you still want to make love?" Pecking her lips.

"Oh yes!" And she kisses him back.

He takes her in his arms, and gently kisses down her neck, to her breasts. As she moans, he kisses back up her neck, and takes her lips in a passionate kiss.

Later as Dan's eyes flicker open, he notices that it is still dark. He tries to look at his watch, but has to get his lighter, and flick it. Three o'clock. He sits up, and looks at Shelly. He puts on his cloths, and shaking her, gently wakes her. "Get dressed so we can take you home." He gets up and walks to near the tree where he last saw Jake. He whistles softly.

Jake opens his eyes as he hears a whistle. Dan whistled again. "What's up?" He asks as he puts on his pants, and stands.

"It's three o'clock, man. We'd better get these girls home."

"Three huh? Okay. We're moving." He wakes Jessie by kissing her, and shaking her gently.

"Hmmm?" She mumbles as she opens her eyes.

He kisses her again. "We have to get you girls home."

She starts to get up and sits right back down. Putting her hands to her head. "Ohhh, my head." She moaned.

It's Time My Darling

"Let me help you." As he gently pulls her to her feet and holds her close.

Smiling up at him, "I'm okay now. Let me get dressed."

"Do I have to?" As he looked her over.

"Yes you have to." Standing on her toes and pecking his lips. "Besides, if mother doesn't hear us come in, you can come to my room."

He releases her, and finishes dressing himself. Gathering the blanket, and taking her hand, walks to the car. Smiling at her, he said, "I'll have to get you drunk more often."

"Why?" She asks smiling back at him.

"You were quite aggressive." He pulled her close and kissed her. "But I liked that, you're my kind of woman."

"Well…" She blushes a little. "You make me feel that way." She leans into him, and raises her lips to his.

Shelly, and Dan came strolling over, arm in arm. Shelly looks at Jessie and asks her, "How's your head?"

"Thumping." She answered simply. "Next time I'll take it easy."

"Me too!" Shelly exclaimed.

They helped the girls into the car, and Jake sits there for a moment. "I think we should just stay here for the rest of the night."

"No, Jake. I have to go home. We can do this again sometime." Looking at the others. "Right? We can do it again?"

"Sure," Dan said as he looked at Shelly.

"I'll do it. I had a lot of fun."

"We could camp." Jake offered. "I have a tent." He touched Jessie's cheek. "I'd like to spend the whole night with you."

Placing her hand over his, she moved it to her lips. "Okay. I'll do it." She said against it.

As he starts the car, he says, "I knew there was something I wanted to tell you." As he backs around, "the other day I was over at Salinas, and I saw Lynn. And you'll never guess who she was with?"

"Who?" Jessie asked as she gave him the eye.

"You know Lena's fiancé, Jack?"

"No!?" Shelly said shocked, and dismayed.

"Yes! And they were coming out of a motel six!

Shelly inhaled and covered her mouth. "But she is Lena's best friend!"

"Well if that's being a best friend, Lena doesn't need any enemies. Right?" Jake looks back at her.

"Poor Lena." Jessie said sadly. She turned to Shelly. "And you were afraid she'd go after Dan."

Dan scoffed at that. "It wouldn't do her any good."

Shelly looked at him, and smiled. "You've just made me very happy."

He hugged her close. "Don't ever doubt me, babe! I love you."

Jessie smiled at her. "Told you." Sighing deeply as she turns back around. "Now what do we do? Lena's wedding is in three weeks. Her rehearsal in next week, I believe."

"We're not doing anything." Jake said firmly. "I feel bad for her, but it's not our place to interfere."

"But wouldn't you want to know if I was doing it to you?" Jessie asked, a little perturbed.

"I hope I never have to find out." He answered her simply.

"Of course, you never will." She pushes on his arm. "I gave myself to you, because I want it to be for life!" She sits and pouts. "I still say we should tell her."

"I don't know, Jessie. She might hold a grudge against you for being the one to tell her." Shelly shakes her head.

"Maybe that jerk she's supposed to be marrying will change his mind and tell her before it goes that far." Jake said in anger.

"I pray that he will." Shelly says with tears in her eyes.

Dan wipes them away. "I know, this is sad news, babe, but you can't let it ruin things for you."

"I know," she answers sadly. "I'm sorry, but, we've known her almost as long as the rest of the crowd. And why she ever chose Lynn as her best friend is beyond me!" She said in anger.

"She has always been a back stabber, and any man that she could get, she did. No matter who they were." Jessie said in disgust. "You weren't one of them were you?" Looking at him.

"You've got to be kidding?!" Jake was taken aback. "Honestly, Jessica. How could you even suggest that?"

"We didn't always go steady." She defended herself.

"No, but if you stop and think about it, I never took anyone but you out."

"I know, Jake, and I'm sorry. I shouldn't have asked you that."

They rode in silence for the better part of the way home. The sadness they felt for Lena weighed heavy on their minds. Each of them hoping it never happened to them.

Jake walked her to her door, and stepped inside to say goodnight.

"Aren't you staying for a while?" She put her arms around his neck. "I'm really sorry for what I said. That was unfair."

"It's already forgotten." He kisses her. "I had just better go home. "I have to drop Shelly off, and run Dan home. But I had a good time today."

Smiling at him. "I'm glad it turned out the way it did. I feel safe about my mother and Dave now, and I enjoyed another wonderful night of sex with my man." Blushing at her boldness.

"I am your man, and don't you ever forget it!" He kisses her tenderly.

"I wont. And that's a promise I can keep." She kissed him back. "I love you."

"I love you too. I'll call you in the morning. I think I'm going to take the day off so we can do some serious talking. Okay?"

"Alright." She sight deeply. "I'll see you then."

He kissed her again. "Night, love."

"Are you sure you want to leave?" As she ran her fingers over his lips.

"You're making this awfully hard for me, Jessica." He kisses her passionately. "Now, yes. I have to go."

"Night," she pouted.

He hesitated at the door. "I'll call you."

She closes the door, and locks it, and watches him get into the car, and pull away. Sighing, she goes to the kitchen to get a glass of juice. She notices a note on the table, and picks it up. It was a note from her mom. Sweetie, I've gone to Dave's for the night. See you in morning. Love, mother. Jessie smiled to herself. She climbs the steps slowly. All of a sudden, she didn't feel so hot. Maybe she shouldn't have drank that juice. She ran for the toilet and heaved. She raises up slowly, and leans against the wall. Feeling dizzy, and none to steady, she sits on the edge of the tub. She sits there for a few moments to be sure she isn't going to be sick again, and then, rinses her mouth out, and goes to her room. She gets undressed, and almost as soon as her head hit's the pillow, she's out.

She's in the mist again, and she's running, but she feels something different. She feels lost. She feels an intense dread, and wants to cry, and scream at the same time. Then she feels it's presence, because, she gets this terrible fear, sending chills all over her body. She tries to run faster. Run, run she tells herself, then she hears the breathing. Heavy breathing, the hissing and growling all around her. She's running for her life. Then the mist clears, and she sees the house, but she has no idea where she is at. She sees a house, but it's not her safe haven. She hears a large growl, and turns to see this form standing there. It was no longer floating, but standing on two feet. It had on men's clothing, and over top of it was the pick polka dot dress. It had on one woman's shoe, and one mans shoe, and the blonde wig. It slowly walked toward her, and as it got closer, she could see the blood all over the front of the dress, and on it's hands and face. She could do nothing but back up, because, she somehow knew the house behind her was her doom. In his left hand was a knife. It also was covered in blood. She had never known fear as she did this moment, but she also felt that she needed to be strong. She stopped moving, and stood perfectly still. Her heart pounding, and sweat rolling down her face. It stopped also. It started laughing. Mad, intense laughing. Then it raised the knife, and stabbed at her as she closed her eyes. Nothing happened, and she opened her eyes to find it gone. She turned frantically to try to find it. She turns several times, but doesn't see it. She can feel it as she turns around and around, trying desperately to find it. Where are you? She thinks. Wanting to scream. She hears and sees nothing but silence. She turns back to the house, and starts to run toward it, when it appears suddenly, and blocks her path. Menacingly, it stalks toward her, and she turns to run the other way, back into the mist. Then she does what she was trying so hard not to do. She falls. She rolls over, and looks at it, as it stalks slowly toward her, laughing at her, and sneering. She scoots backward, and tries to get up, but it knocks her down again. She lay still, and her eyes widened in fright, as it came over her and knelt down. Goo dripping from it's mouth, as it bent to her face. She turned her face away. It took the knife tip, and placing it against her cheek, he pushed her face back to his. His evil eyes staring into her. Then he pulls back, and stares at her heaving breast. She closes her eyes, and looks away again, not wanting to see that thing look at her that way. Goo drips on her face, as he lowers his to hers. She tries to scream, but nothing comes out, as she pushes on his chest, and rolls him off of her. Scrambling to her feet, she runs back into the dense mist. She can hear his heavy breathing, and runs faster. As the mist starts to subside, she sees her house, and Jake is standing on the porch with his arms outstretched to her. She hears it's insane laughter, as she looks back and sees it standing there, Jakes arms enclosed around her. Opening her eyes slowly, she lays there and tries to catch her breath. She puts her hands to her face to see if there was any goo, or slobber, or what ever it was on her. There is nothing but sweat. She shuddered at the thought of that thing touching her. Rolling over to get out of her bed, she notices that it is bright outside. She looked at the clock, and seeing that it was eight, decided to get up.

****

IV

"Down in the kitchen, she tries to decide if she should try to eat something, or pass. She decided she'd make a bowl of cereal and toast. She reached for the juice, but pulled her hand back, not quite sure how her stomach would handle it this morning. The cereal tasted awful, so she didn't eat it. The toast was enough, she realized, for the way she felt. She went back to her room, and made her bed, and fixed her hair, then went out to sit on the swing. She decided to read some in the books, so she goes back in to get them, and grabs the phone also. She was reading about dreams, when the phone rings. "Hello."

"What are you doing? You sound preoccupied." Jake asked her. "I'm reading," she answered softly.

"How do you feel this morning?" She could hear laughter in his voice.

"Jake, are you laughing at me?"

"Not at all."

"Liar!" She laughed at him. "You should have stayed. My mother wasn't here."

"She wasn't? Where did she go?"

"She spent the night with Dave. I'm sure she went to work from there 'cause she didn't come home this morning."

"This is serious, isn't it?"

"It looks that way. Are you coming over?" She sighed.

"We have to put a muffler on this car, and then we will."

"We really have to talk." She sounded very serious.

"Did you have another one of those dreams?" He asked concerned.

"Yes, but this was different." She sighed again. "So, whenever you can get here, please do! Okay?"

"I'll have Dan call Shelly, and we'll be over as soon as we can." He assured her. "We'll see you in a bit."

"Bye."

"Jessica?" He lowered his voice.

"What?" She smiled to herself.

"I love you," he said in a husky voice.

"I love you too," she whispered back. "Bye, Jake."

"Bye, Jessie."

She's still smiling as she lays the phone down. She's staring into the sky, when she sees a little bird come and sit on the branch in front of her house. Looking at it as it chirps, she asks. "Are you my little guardian angel?" It chirps again and flies away. She smiles as she picks up the book again, and starts to read. She is feeling restless this morning, so she goes back into the house and, deciding that she was hungry, fixed herself an egg and toast. Do I want coffee, she thinks. After pondering for a moment, she puts some on. She is buttering her toast when the phone rings.

"Hello," she answered preoccupied.

"Good morning, sweetie," her mother said cheerfully.

"Good morning, mother."

"I thought I'd call, and let you know where I am."

"You're at work, aren't you?"

Her mother laughed. "No, I'm afraid not. I didn't feel like going in today, so I did something I never do. I called off."

"Mother, shame on you!" Jessie laughed.

"I know, I feel so naughty." She giggled.

Jessie laughed at her. "Oh, mother, you're so funny."

"Maybe I am, but I feel I deserve a day off. Besides, Dave has to go somewhere today, and I'm going with him."

"Mmmm, I see." She teased. "Well you have a good day." "I will, and I'll be home later tonight."

"Love you, mother."

"I love you too. And you be good today."

"Mother? Before you hang up, do you have time for one question?"

"Of course, sweetie. What's wrong?"

"Well… Jake was over to Salinas the other day, and he saw Lynn with Lena's Fiancé. They were coming out of a motel. Do I tell her?"

"Oh, sweetie, this is terrible. Poor Lena." She sighed deeply. "No, you shouldn't tell her, Jessie. I know you probably think that it's not right, but sometimes the person who tells becomes the other persons object of hate. It's odd how that works, but it's a known fact, that the one who tells takes the brunt of the others anger."

Jessie says, "but, mother, somebody has to do it!"

"No, Jessica. It's not your responsibility. Listen to me. I know she's your friend, but that doesn't mean you have to do anything. Understand?" She said in exasperation.

Jessie sighed deeply. "I guess you are right."

"Keep your nose out of it!" Her mother repeated. "Now I have to get off of here. And, listen to me."

"Yes, mother. Love you."

"Love you too. Bye."

She lays the phone down, and finishes her breakfast. Her mind is not wanting to follow the advice she was given. She knew that she somehow had to forget this terrible thing. She poured a cup of coffee, and went back out to sit on the swing. She is sitting there, feeling very low, when the others pull up.

"Hi, Jessie," Shelly is positively beaming this morning.

"Hi," Jessie smiled at her.

"Hey, what's wrong with you?" Jake asks as he sits beside her.

"Nothing." Smiling sadly. "I was just thinking, that's all."

He kisses her. She kisses him back.

I hear your mother stayed at Dave's last night?" Shelly teased.

"How about that? Get this. She didn't go to work today."

"How'd you find that out?" Jake asked her.

"She called me this morning. She said that she didn't go to work, and that she was going somewhere with Dave. She'll be home later tonight."

"Ohhh," Shelly teased. "I does think your mom is stricken."

"Shelly, you're funny. Does think?" Jessie laughed at her. "Does anybody want coffee? There's a pot in here if you do."

"Yes, I'll have some." He takes ahold of Jessie's hand and pulls her up.

She laughs as she follows him into the house. She was getting them cups when the phone rang. "Hello."

"Jessica? This is Donna. Is your mother alright?"

"Oh yeah. She's fine." Jessie's voice is full of laughter.

"Why then did she call off today? I couldn't believe it."

"Me either," Jessie laughed. "But I guess she entitled to day off once in a while."

"It's just so strange not to see her here." She lowered her voice. "You know what else? Alice is really upset that she didn't come in today. She was slamming things around on her desk, and said something about her being a floozy."

"Really? That's odd, don't you think?"

"You tell your mother to be careful, Jessica. Okay?" She whispered. "I'm going to get off of here, and go back to work. I'll talk to you later." Her voice had meaning.

"Bye, Donna. And thanks." She turned to the others. "Wait till you hear this!" She was excited. "That was Donna, from my mom's office. She said that Alice is really upset that my mom called off today. That she was slamming things around on her desk, and called my mom a floozy!"

"What?" Shelly exclaimed.

"Yeah. Can you believe that?" She asks exasperated.

Jake shook his head. "You know what, guys. Maybe we'd better start watching your mom close. It sounds like that woman is about to crack. I mean, if she's that bold about it at the office."

Jessie shuddered. "You know what, Jake? I think you're right, because I had this horrible dream. I saw that thing again, and this time it had it's legs. It was dressed in men's clothing, and had that polka dot dress on over top of them. It had on one woman's shoe, and one man's. It was covered in blood. The dress, it's face, the knife it was holding, and it was running down it's arm. I fell, and it knelt over me." She shuddered again. "Those evil eyes staring a hole in me, and that menacing laugh. Dripping goo all over my face." She touched it and made a face. "Yuck!"

"Is that why you said we had to talk?"

"Yep," as she sat on his lap. "I feel strongly that something is about to happen. We need to ride out by her house to see if it was the one in my dream. Remember, I couldn't look the last time, but she's at the office now. So it'll be safe for us."

"You dreamt of her house?" Dan asked, shaking his head in wonder.

"I don't know. That's why it's so important for me to go out there. I did dream of a house, and it wasn't ours. I think that's where whatever is going to happen, does."

"And you think we can stop it?" Jake asked, not so sure.

"I believe that we can. We have a warning system, you might say. That being my dreams. So far, everything points to Alice. I think we need to see if we can find out anything about her. Why did I see it dressed in men's clothing, with a woman's over top? Could it be a cross dresser? Did it change itself to be a woman? And if so, why?" She sighed. "What if it took someone else's identity?" She put her hand to her mouth.

"What?" Shelly asked, worried at her expression.

"What if he's a man from my mother's past?"

"Now that's scary!" Dan said.

Jessie gets up, and getting the phone, dials a number.

"What are you doing?" Jake asked, leery of her actions.

She held up her finger. "Could I speak to Donna, please?"

"Hello," Donna answered.

"Donna, this is Jessie. What hand does Alice write with?"

"She's left handed. Why?"

"I knew it!" She was excited. "I dreamt it, but I had to be sure of it. Thanks, Donna."

"You're welcome. And remember, if you need anything, call me."

"Okay. Bye." Laying the phone down, she said, "now you see? She's left handed. Whenever I see that thing, it's always got the knife in it's left hand." She sits on Jakes lap again. "Now do you believe me?"

"I've believed you for some time now." Jake said truthfully.

"Yeah, me too." Dan agreed.

"Okay, so let's get on the computer, and see if we can find anything out about Miss Alice Watson."

They go to her room. "Go ahead, Jake. You could always work it better than me."

"How do we go about this?" Shelly asked her. "You have to have a category to go into, don't you?"

"I never thought of that. Okay, I'll call Donna again." She rolls her eyes. "She's going to get tired of me calling her."

"I'll warm this up while you do that." Jake said, as he sits.

She bounced down the steps, two at a time. She dialed the number, and stood there tapping her foot as it rang several times. "Come on," she said impatiently. Finally someone picked up. "May I speak to Donna?"

"Hello," Donna finally answers.

"Donna, I hate to bother you again. Oh yeah, this is Jessica. Is there any way you could get me Alice's social security number?"

"What do you need that for?"

"Well, we're going to go online to find out anything about her. Did she ever say where she came from? Her home town, or state maybe?"

"Jessica, I wish you'd reconsider. I'd hate for her to find out about this." She whispered.

"Is she near you?"

"Yes, but hold on. I'll see if I have that." She put Jessie on hold for a few moments. "Okay. I was able to get it. Ready?" She said in a low voice.

"Go ahead," Jessie answered her.

"Two nine one - Zero four - seven three six one. And she was originally from South Carolina."

"That's where my mom was from. I wonder? Okay. Thanks, Donna."

"You be sure and let me know what going on." Donna ordered her.

"I will. As soon as we find something concrete out."

"And tell your mother to call me tonight."

"Alright, Donna. Bye."

She flew back up the steps. "I've got it. And guess what else? She did come from my mom's state. I'll wager you, it's the same home town too." She was excited now.

"What's the name?"

"Beaufort, South Carolina."

"Okay. So we'll tap into states, and see what we can do."

He types in the state. South Carolina. The city. Beaufort. Population, nine thousand five hundred and seventy-three. Now what's her name again?"

"Alice Watson." Jessie lays the social security number before him. "Social security number, two nine one - zero four - seven three six one."

"How about her age?"

"Well my mom is forty-one. Try that and see."

He types it in, and searching, came up on the screen. They read the as it prints out. No person found in that area. Person by that name in Edisto Beach. Deceased. No further information available.

"Wow!" Jake leans back in the chair. "This is intense!"

"I knew there had to be something wrong. I'm telling you that she is an it. Or a man." She finishes excitedly. "I'll bet you a dime to a dollar that it's a man, and he knew my mother. And for some ungodly reason, wants to hurt her.

"Then we're going to have to talk to your mother. Find out if there was any one person that might be out to even a score." Jake offered.

"I know your dad has a friend on the police department, Jake. Do you think, maybe, he would be able to get him to find out what happened to Alice Watson? How she died maybe?" Dan asked him.

"I can ask him. That sure would be nice to know."

"I hope she wasn't murdered," Shelly whispered.

"That's probably a bit far fetched, Shelly." Jake said. He gets up. "Okay, Let's go talk to my dad."

Jessie hesitated. "But we'll have to tell him everything."

"Probably. But my dad is a good guy. He'll listen to what I have to say."

"I wouldn't be able to face him again if I thought he'd think of me nuts." She exclaimed in despair.

Jake laughs at her. "You convinced us, didn't you.?"

"Yes," she answered slowly.

She still hesitates. "Really, Jake, this is not something you tell just anyone. Admit it. You probably thought me crazy when you first heard it."

He takes her in his arms. "I did not think you crazy. And I was amazed you even talked about it. That made me think you were telling the truth." He kissed her gently. "I know my dad. Now come on, time's a wasting."

"Oh, alright," she gives in. "But if I even, for one minute, think he is not believing any of this, then I'm leaving."

"Deal." As he puts his arms around her.

His dad was still in the garage when they walk in. "Can we talk to you for a minute, dad?"

"Sure," as he closes the ledger he was looking at. He looks at the others. "Hi, kids."

"Hi, Mr. Lansing." They say together.

"Okay. What do you need?" He smiled at them.

"Well, nothing really, except a small favor." Jake clears his throat. "You see. We need you to ask Mike if he can find out how someone died for us?"

"I see. Can I ask why? I think I should know something, anything if I'm to ask that kind of favor."

"Well…" Clearing his throat again, "it's a long story, but we think Jessica's mother might be in danger. And we went online today to find a person, and it came back deceased. Yet a person working with Jessie's mom has the same name. Is from the same state, and about the same age."

He leans forward in his chair. "Your mother thinks she in danger?" He points as Jessie.

"No," shaking her head. "I think she's in danger."

"Why?" He asked simply.

She looked at Jake. Her eyes begging for help.

"About a month ago, Jessie started having these dreams. Bad one's. And then when the people she saw came into her mother's life. He sells life insurance. This woman at work sent him to Jessie's mom, and some strange things have been happening. Even the other women at work are concerned. They begged Carol to be careful. This person is nasty they say."

"I see." He leans back again, and tapping his pencil says, "If I do this, and Mike wants to talk to you, you'll do it?"

Jake looks at Jessie. "He'll listen, Jessica. He's not a skeptic like most people. As long as he thinks your on the up and up, he'll help you."

Jessie straightened her shoulders. "Alright, Jake. Let's do it." She sighs. "I know beyond a doubt, my mother is in trouble, and I must do this."

"I'll call him and see if he'll do this on what I know." He picks up the phone, dials, and waits. "Janet, this is George Lansing. Is Mike around?"

"I'll ring his office. Hold on."

"Hello, George. What do you need?"

"Do you think you could find out how a person died for me?"

"Should I ask why?"

"It's very important to me. If you need to know more, then I can stop in."

"I'll take your word on it. Give me the name."

Jake handed him the paper with the information. He, intern read it to Mike, and asked him not to say anything.

"I'll see what I can do, and call you back."

"Okay. I'll wait to hear from you." He looks at them and says, "depending on what he finds out, he might want to talk with you."

"That's okay. We'll hang around until you hear from him. I hope he has something to tell us." "Yeah, me too." Jessie sighed. She looks around the shop, and spots and old car on the far side of the shop. "I like that car." Pointing at it.

"That's the mercury I was telling you about. Want to see it up close?"

"Yeah!" She exclaimed.

Jake takes her hand, and leads her over to it. "Look inside."

She bent over and peered in. "Wow!"

"Nice isn't it?"

"Yes. Is it your?"

"Not yet, but I hope soon. I'll take you for a ride in it if you want."

"I want!" She laughed.

They hear the phone ring, and taking her hand, they go back to the office.

"Hello," as he listens intently. "I see," he pauses. "I can explain." He pauses again. "Sure, come over." He listens intently, frowning. "Okay. I'll be in the office." He hung up the phone. "He is coming over. I'll let him talk to you kids. It seem you might have opened an old case."

They look at one another, and Jake squeezed her hand. "It looks like you were right."

She felt such terrible dread. "I know what he's going to say. That woman was murdered. And she probably had something to do with it."

Jake takes her in his arms, and holds her gently. "No matter what we find out, Jessica, don't be discouraged. I think we can still help your mother." He pulls her close. "Okay?"

She shook her head, not trusting herself to speak. She felt this terrible urge to cry.

Jake's dad looks at her. "You'll have to tell me what sort of dream you had, that could open up a murder case."

She looks at Jake. "Well, you'll probably hear it word for word if that policeman has to know how we came to ask about Alice Watson."

They see a car pull in. "That's Mike." Jake told her.

Jessie could feel her nerves jump, and stared at him intensely as he got out of the car. She never took her eyes off of his face.

"Calm down," Jake whispered in her ear. "It'll be okay.'

George greets him, and shakes his hand. "You know my son Jake." He offers his hand. "And Dan." He shakes his hand. "And these two young ladies are Jessica, and Shelly." He offers his hand to them as well.

They all sit down.

"I don't know how you came up with this name, but it's a murder case from South Carolina. Care to talk to me?" He looks at George with meaning.

"Those are the four you need to talk to." As he points at the kids.

Nodding. "Who is the one asking all the questions about Alice Watson?"

"We all were." Jake spoke up.

"Why?" Mike asked simply.

Jessie took a deep breath. "Alright. It's all my fault." She clears her throat. "Please listen to what I have to say. All of it before you cut in." She sighs. "About a month ago, I started having very bad dreams. I see this man in a pink polka dot dress, and he's chasing me. He almost gets me, when my house appears, and I touch the porch, and wake up. Then a few nights later, I dream it again, and he's dressed the same, only this time he has a blonde wig on. The next time is the same, but he grabs my shirt just as I touch the porch and wake up. Then, that very day, a man knocks on our door asking for my mother. I froze in my tracks. You can imagine my horror, because it was him. He was there to see mother. Here he's an insurance man, and mother was buying extra coverage. When Shelly and I had the chance, we asked her how she had met him, and she told us about Alice

Watson sending him over. What's strange about this is that she never liked my mother. Mother said that she gives her the willies, and that she treats her down right awful. The girls at the office told me to tell mother to watch herself. Especially since her and Dave hit it off. When I called the office today to see if a friend of mother's would give me Alice's social security number, she did it willingly. And she begged me to be careful, and tell mother to please call her. It seems Alice went into a rage, because mother and Dave are together.

"Who's Dave?" Mike asked her.

"The insurance man. He's dating my mom."

"I see," he frowned. "This doesn't bother you?"

"No," shaking her head vehemently. "He's on the up and up."

"Go on then," Mike said.

"Then I have this dream, where I'm being chased by this thing. It has on men's clothing, but over top is the pink polka dot dress. It has on the blonde wig, and on one foot is a man's shoe, and on the other, a woman's. It tries to attack me, and I notice it has a knife in it's left hand. If was dripping with blood. There was blood all over the clothes it had on. I noticed that it held the knife in it's left hand, so I called mother's friend, and asked her what hand Alice used. She told me the left hand. Can you believe it? That's when I found out her number, and where she was from. I guess she's only been here a couple of years. Then I had Jake go online to see if we could find out about her, and the rest you know."

Shaking his head, Mike said earnestly, "unbelievable!"

"You had no knowledge of any of this?" George asked dumbfounded.

"No, sir. I had nothing until the dreams started. I feel it's a warning to protect my mother."

"Where was the real Alice killed?" Dan asked.

"She worked in a mental hospital. This is the sad part. The day that she disappeared was her day off. She had stopped to see one of the patients. She had grown fond of her, and brought in a book of pictures on animals. She loved them I guess. Anyhow, she was seen leaving the building, so they thought, and never seen again. It turns out, it wasn't her at all, but a patient who somehow got her, and murdered her, and took her identity. A week later, they found Alice stuffed in the back of the linen closet. She had been strangled." He opened a book. "I'd like you to look at some pictures, and see if you can pick out the one who looks like Alice now."

"I don't know," Jessie hesitates. "I've only seen her once. Can I ask you something?"

"Okay." Mike answered her.

"Is this person a male?" Knowing the answer before she even heard it.

"Yes, he is. Alice was a tall woman, so it wasn't hard for him to be her."

"I told you, Shelly. That's why the man's in a dress."

"What's his name?" Shelly asked him.

"Allen Walters. Hence Alice Watson." He finished, as Jessie looked at the pictures. She took her time and studied them, knowing that the think in her dream was one of them. On the fifth page, she covered her mouth and stared.

"Did you see something?" Mike asked her.

She pointed at a man with dark hair, and dark eyes, that even in the picture, stared holes through her. "That's the one in my dreams."

"You can tell that?" Jake asked in amazement.

"I'm sure of it. Those eyes are what I know." She didn't waver a bit in her decision.

"One more question," Dan said. "Where was he from?"

"Beaufort, South Carolina." Looking at Jessie for a long moment. "He was put into the hospital right after he got out of high school. All those years, he had been a model patient. What made him do this is a mystery."

"That's where my mother was from. How old is he?"

"I believe forty-two."

"See, Shelly, mother is forty-one." She stood up. "I told you. I just knew it was somebody from her past. But what was his reason for doing this?"

"He's a sick man. The reason he was put there to begin with, was for setting a house on fire with the people sleeping inside. Then he tried to run over another woman. Seems these girls all had the same friends. There was three in particular that he chased all the time. Two of them was a Jamie, and Anne. The third, he never got to try to hurt, because she was put away."

"And that third party was named Carol. Right?" Jessica stated as though she knew the answer.

"Jamie he tried to burn, Anne he tried to run over, and Carol was spared."

"My mother!" She breathed out. "Oh, Jake, what are we going to do? We have to stop him!"

"Whoa, little lady! You're not doing anything!" Mike stressed.

Jessie stared at him.

"You listen to me. Has nothing I said sunk into your head? You picked him out!"

She was pale. "I'm sorry. It's just that, where my mother is concerned, I act."

"Without thinking, I might add." Jake said quickly.

She smiled sheepishly.

"Now, tell me where your mother works."

"At Jacobs and Jacobs Law Offices."

He smirked at that. "Imagine that. Working in a law office when you're a murderer, and escaped mental patient."

"She, I mean he, obviously hid it well." Dan spoke up.

"To get by with it for two years is an accomplishment alright. If he hadn't decided to do something against you mother, we might never have got him."

"You don't have him yet," George offered quietly.

"No, you're right, but that's about to change." He asked Jake, "do you know where he lives?"

"Yes. At least we think we do. Out by the lake. Do you want us to take you there?"

"That's not such a good idea. Just give us the general direction, and we'll find it."

"Go out to the lake, and follow the road to the right, all the way back to the last house. It's a cottage style that sits back in by itself." Jake told him.

"You kids stay out of the way, and leave the detective work to us." Mike ordered and looked directly at Jessie. "No if ands or buts about it. Do I make myself clear?"

"Yes sir," they all said together.

George stood and offered his hand to Mike. "Thanks for coming out and listening. Who'd have thought a thing like this could happen?"

"You just never know," Mike said shaking is head. "I guess the Lord works in mysterious ways after all."

"And we are testament to that." Jake agreed.

"I'll be in touch." As he walked to the door. Turning back to Jessie, "by the way. Where is your mother?"

She went somewhere with Dave today. She didn't say where though."

"If she calls, tell her to stay away until we get Allen."

"Okay." She turns to Jake. "Maybe we should stick close to the house. I want to be there if she happens to call."

Jake looks at his dad. "I'll be at your house, dad, if you need me for anything."

His dad called him aside and said, "you stay close to her. She is going to need a lot of support until this guy is caught, and she knows for a fact her mom is safe."

"You can bet on that, dad. I wont leave her side."

Back at her house, Jessie lets them in, and goes straight to the caller ID. Nothing from her mom, but there was a call from Donna. She looked at Jake. "Donna called. I wonder if something is wrong?" She picked up the phone and dialed, "May I speak to Donna, please?"

"Hello," Donna answered.

"Donna, this is Jessica. You called while I was out?"

"Thank God you called back! After I talked to you, and then you called back and asked for her information. She got so agitated, that she left work. She must have been listening, and heard me give it to you."

"Oh no!" Jessie wailed.

"What's wrong?" Jake asked concerned.

"Donna thinks Alice heard her giving me the information on her this morning, and she left work."

"That's not good. She's forewarned, and she's had enough time to leave the area." Dan said very discouraged.

"Thanks, Donna. And you watch yourself when you leave work today."

"I will, dear. You be careful too."

Jessie replaced the phone. "Can you believe that? She had to have been eavesdropping. She probably heard everything Donna told me this morning."

"She's had, I mean he's had enough time to be long gone. They'll never get him." Shelly shuddered at the thought.

"The dream this morning." Jessie turned pale. "Where he was covered with blood." She went into Jake's arms. "What if he knew where my mother and Dave were going today? What if he gets them, and kills them before he gets caught?"

"Don't think that way, honey." Jake holds her close. "You have to stay positive about this. Okay?" Kissing the top of her head.

She looked at him with sad eyes. "I can't lose my mother too, Jake. I can't." Burying her face in his chest.

He rocks her. "Hey, hey. Come on now. You can't think like that. Besides, she's with Dave. That should count for something."

"Maybe we should call that Mike we just talking to." Dan spoke up.

"I'm sure he'll be calling here." Jake answered simply.

"I wouldn't be afraid he's long gone by now." Shelly said.

"You know? I wonder if he was that intent on revenge, or whatever against your mother, If he went after the other two woman?"

"What could they have done that was so bad, for this guy to try and burn one of them, and run the other over?" Dan mused.

"Who says they did anything? You know how the sick mind works. It sees or hears what it wants, and some kill because of it." Jake stated.

"That is very scary," Shelly shuddered.

Jake leads Jessie to the couch. "How about some coffee?"

She smiled sadly. "That sounds good. I'll make some." Getting up.

Jake pushes her back onto the couch. "No you won't. Just sit there and look pretty. I'll make it." Smiling lovingly at her.

"This should be good." Shelly teased.

"I make a pretty mean pot of coffee," Jake said to her.

"That's what I'm afraid of." She smirked.

Jake pushed her as she walked by. "Sit down, and shut up."

She plopped onto the couch laughing.

"He does make good coffee. I should know." Dan told her.

"Does that mean you can too?" She smiled sweetly at him.

"I sure does. His mom was a good teacher."

"So," turning her attention to Jessie, "Jessie, do you think you still want to major in psychology? I mean, this could lead to serious stuff."

"I know," she sighed. "But you have to understand that if even one person can be helped, it is worth risks involved. I think it will be very rewarding."

"I'm sure it is, but you also have to think about how our society has changed today. There is more sickness out there, Jessie, than at any other time in history." Dan said frankly. "Isn't that sad? That's exactly why I must do it. I have to try and find a was to stop the progression of this sickness. There has to be a way."

"Listen to us," Shelly laughs. "Talking like a bunch of old fogies.

Jake came back into the room. "Why don't we get some lunch for us, Dan? And then maybe, after a bit, go to the beach, and hang out."

"We can't go anywhere. What if my mother would call?"

"Stop and think about this, Jessie. Do you really think that your mom is going to call you? Does she normally do that?" Jake asked her.

"You're right. She called me this morning. She knows she doesn't have to worry about me, so she probably won't call back."

"Especially if she's having a good time," Shelly said quietly.

"So we'll eat, and then we'll go relax." Jake stated. "And I'll not argue with you about it, Jessie. You're going."

"Besides, Jessie, the cops are watching his place, I'm sure. If he even sniffs, they'll get him!" Dan said to ease her mind.

"Okay, okay! You guys win," she laughs. "I'll go with you."

"And enjoy yourself," Shelly smiles back at her.

"Coffee should be done. You two sit tight, wile we go get the food." Jake said.

"Aye captain," Shelly salutes. They all laugh at him.

"One of these days, Shelly," as he shakes his fist at her.

She cowers, and pretends fright, but as he walks out the door, she whispers, "men are such babies."

He poked his head back in. "I heard that." "No you didn't." Shelly answered.

Jessie went to the kitchen, and poured her coffee. "Did you get much sleep after they took you home last night?"

"Not really. I got a little sick, and my head hurt. Then when I laid down, my head spun. When I got up this morning, all I ate was a piece of toast." Shelly touched her stomach.

"Me too. I don't think I like champagne." Jessie made a face.

"It wasn't so much the drink, as it was we drank too much. We're not used to that, Jessie."

"You got that right." Jessie laughs. "Next time, if there is a next time, I'll be sure and moderate how much I drink."

"That goes for me also. I don't like the feeling you get afterwards." Shelly makes a face.

Sitting at the table, looking out the window, Jessie muses, "I wonder if he did hurt those other two woman? I know that mother used to keep in touch with them. Then the one moved to France."

"Well, you can probably bet that she's okay. But what about the other one?"

Jessie shuddered. "I hope she's okay."

"Foods here," Shelly said as the guys walk in.

"Smells good. I am kind of hungry." Jessie sniffed the air.

"Whoppers and fries. Is that okay?" Dan asked, as they set the bags on the table.

"Our favorite," Shelly sniffs the air.

Jessie got their coffee, and pulled her chair next to Jake's.

He smiled into her eyes, and giving her a peck on the lips asked, "better now?"

"Yes," she smiled back. "Shelly and I were just talking about mother's friends. One of them moved to France. Anne, I believe it was. So she is probably alright, huh?"

"You know what, Jake? You do make good coffee." Shelly ate crow.

"Glad you noticed." He looked back at Jessie. "So how did you feel after we left this morning?"

"Not so hot. I drank some juice, and I think it made me sick."

"Orange juice?"

She shook her head. "It came right back up."

"You never drink orange juice when your tipsy." Jake laughs at her.

"I didn't know," she defended herself. "And I wasn't tipsy, I was drunk!"

Dan laughs at her. "I saw you take a few spills. If I hadn't had my hand full with Shelly, I'd have died laughing at you."

"She was pretty funny, wasn't she?" Jake eyes danced with laughter.

"Don't even start, mister. It was your fault to begin with." She said with mock anger.

Dan says laughing, "we learned one thing. You two can't hold your drinks."

"You had better watch your mouth, mister." Jessie's eyes shot daggers.

Dan looks at Jake. "I think I'm being threatened.

"It sounds that way." He trying to keep a straight face.

Jessie looks at Shelly, and waves her brows, "when they least expect it."

Dan grads his chest. "Help me," he whispers hoarsely. "I'm so frightened, I'm having a heart attack."

Jessie threw French fries at him.

They all laugh, and Dan says meekly, "I'm sorry. I shouldn't joke it that way."

"It's all in clean fun." Jake replied.

"Let's sit out on the porch." Jessie gets up, and taking the cups, sits them in the sink. "I'll do those later."

Jake throws the bags away, and takes her in his arms. "I haven't really had a chance to kiss you good this morning."

"How about now?" Smiling into his eyes.

He never took his eyes from hers, as he lowered his lips. He kissed her tenderly. His lip lingered on hers for a long moment. She kissed him back.

"That's more like my Jessie," he breathed into her ear.

"Chills. You gave me chills." She giggled.

He smiled at her, "I'd like to give you more than that."

Smiling sweetly, "don't even go there, sweetie. Not yet anyhow."

"Not yet, huh? What if we lose those two?" nodding his head at Dan and Shelly.

"Look at them," she whispered. "I think they're finally learning to be more open."

He smiled. "Are we good teachers or what?" Patting himself on the back.

She smiled too, and taking his hand, leads him outside. He sits on the swing, and she sits on his lap, and leans against him. "I don't really feel like the beach today, Jake. Can't we do something else?"

"Like what?" He kissed her head.

"Can we maybe go for a ride in that car you showed me earlier?"

"You liked that, huh?" Smiling at her.

"Oh yeah. It's awesome." She breathed out.

"I think I can arrange that."

She sighed deeply.

"What was that for?" He kissed her ear.

"I'm just content, I guess." She lays her head on his shoulder.

Dan and Shelly came out and sat down. "Are we doing anything?" Dan asked.

"Jessie would like to take the Mercury out."

"You like that, huh?" Dan smiled, understanding her feelings. "It's a nice car."

"I know it looks nice, but I'd like to find out how it rides. I remember riding in an old Corvette once. I didn't really like it. The ride was rough, and it sat so low to the ground.'

"They're like that. Those old Corvettes." Jake agreed with her.

"I'd like to go for a ride in it too," Shelly said eagerly. I've never ridden in an old car before."

"Okay. That's settled then, we'll do just that." Jake stands up.

Jessie looks up, and taking Jakes hand, pulls him to his car. "Come on. Let's go!"

Jake laughs at her. "There's never a dull moment with you, Jessie. Helping her into the car.

"Boy, you can say that again!" Dan said laughing.

Jessie smiled her sweet smile. "But don't you just love me?"

They look at one another and raise their brows.

"Oh come on, you guy," she said exasperated.

Jake and Dan start laughing at her. "Of course we love you," Jake finally said.

"Yeah," Dan agreed. "I can't imagine what it would be like without you around." He paused, and looked as though he were in deep thought. "But then maybe I can. It would be peaceful, if nothing else." He was trying to keep a straight face, but not doing a very good job of it.

Jessie got up on her knees, and turned to take a swing at him.

He flinched, and fell into Shelly. Laughing at her.

Shelly put her arms around him, "behave yourself, and you won't get hit."

"So there!" Jessie smarted off to him.

They pull into Jakes drive, and his dad is standing there talking with his mother. Jake walks up to him. "Can we take the mercury out for a drive?"

He looked at them for a moment. "No hot Roding, Jake."

"No, sir. Jessie was taken with it, and asked if I'd take her for a ride."

"We'll behave. I promise," she smiled sweetly at him.

He handed over the keys.

"Thanks, dad."

"Where are you going?"

"I think I'll show her that property we looked at the other day."

"Lock up when you get back."

"Yes, sir." Jake takes Jessie's hand. "You're going to like this ride."

She smiled up at him, and turned to his parents, "thank you."

"You're welcome," his dad smiled back.

As Jessie gets into the car, she exclaims, "Shelly, look at this. Isn't it beautiful?"

"I don't know what it is about old cars, but you feel special whenever you're in one."

"Ready?" Jake smiled at her.

Shaking her head emphatically, "let's go!"

He beeps at his parents as he pulls away. "Let's go for a joy ride."

"Why did you tell your dad we are going to the property we were at last night?" Dan asked a little puzzled.

"Because we are." Jake answered simply. "I thought we'd show it to the girls while there is lots of daylight. We can do a little exploring of the property, and then take them to get something to eat." He glanced over his shoulder at Dan. "Is that alright with you?"

"Sure. I don't have a problem with that."

"This car rides so nice," as she slid closer to Jake. "And I like being able to sit next to you."

"Yeah," he put his arm around her, and pulled her closer.

"How about we do a steak tonight? I don't feel like a whopper, or big mac, or anything like that. I'm hungry for a juicy steak." Dan said licking his lips.

"Ummm, that sounds good." Shelly licked her lips too.

"Yeah, I could handle that, or maybe even red lobster." Jake agreed willingly.

"Look at the people looking at your car!" Jessie exclaimed.

"You get used to that." Jake smiled at her. "I told you. There's just something about an old car that makes people stare."

"I guess so," Jessie remarked.

On their way out of town, they heard someone whistle, and looked to see who it was. They see Mike and Jenny, on his bike, waving like crazy at them. Jake beeps at them, and keeps going. "I think they are following us."

"Oh, I hope so. I haven't talked to Jenny for a couple of days, and I'd like to find out how the bonfire went."

"Mike said we missed a hell of a party." Dan said to her.

"When did you see him?" Shelly asked.

"Yesterday. He's working for Jake's dad now."

"You didn't tell me that?" Jessie said accusingly.

Jake shrugs his shoulders. "I didn't think it was important."

"Are you guys that bust, that you need extra help? I'd do it." She pouted.

Jake laughs at that one. "Soon to be Miss Psychologist here? I don't think this is your kind of work."

"I could learn," she pouted. "And stop laughing at me."

He looks at her, his eyes dancing mischievously. "What's the matter, Jessie? Did I step on your toes?"

She looked out the window, and totally ignored him.

"By golly, Jake. I think the cats got her tongue." Dan said in amazement.

She shot him a look, and then smiling sweetly at Jake, "Of course you didn't step on my toes. And no," looking at Dan again, "the cat doesn't have my tongue. I just think it's unfair, that just because I'm a girl, you think I can't do the job."

"I didn't say that," Jake objected.

"In so many words, you did." She shot back at him.

"Sorry, honey, but I just don't see you with grease on your face and hands." Apologizing with his eyes.

She melted. "Oh, you're probably right." She sighed deeply. "I have being type cast."

"I think you should get used to it, Jessie." Shelly offered. "Because you have that certain look about you that causes that sort of reaction."

As Jake turns up the lane, he sees Mike do the same. He parks the car, and help Jessie out, as Mike pulls the bike along side him.

"What's up, man?" Mike asks as he gets off the bike.

"Nothing much. I wanted to show the girls this piece of land up here."

"Do you care if we tag along?"

"Not at all." Jake answered.

Jessie and Shelly hugged Jenny. "We were hoping you'd follow us. I wanted to know about the part the other night. Did any of the red necks show up?"

"Not a one. Maybe they are getting the picture that some of us are tired of their crap. As for the party, it was a blast. An absolute blast. Too bad you didn't come over."

"I know, but Jake and Dan were tired, and we decided to sit at my house. We ordered pizza, and watched Pay Per View.

Probably not as exciting as your night, but we enjoyed being together." Jessie smiled at the last remark.

"Usually I'd prefer that too, but as it turned out, we didn't have not one invasion. I have to tell you though, Lynn and Tom got into this huge fight, and she left really angry." Jenny offered.

"Do you know what it was about?" Shelly looked at Jessie.

"It seems," she lowered her voice, "it seems she's been trying to call her, and she's never home. When he asked her where she has been all of these times, she said at work. He told her she was a liar, and asked her who she was seeing. You should seen the look on her face."

"What was it like?" Jessie asked curiously.

"She turned pale, her eyes got big, and she stuttered bad. And Tom told her he didn't think he wanted to be bothered with her anymore."

"No sir?!" Shelly exclaimed.

Shaking her head, "Yes he did."

Taking her arm, and leading her ahead of the guys. "You swear to God you won't repeat to anyone what I'm going to tell you?" Jessie asked her earnestly.

"Swear to God," as she crosses her heart.

"We know who she's seeing." Jessie whispered.

"Who? And don't you pull none of that changing the subject stuff. Now who?" She repeated.

Jessie looks at Shelly and answers her quietly. "Lena's man."

Jenny put her hand to her mouth. "You've got to be kidding me?!"

Shelly shakes her head. "Afraid not."

"Jack? She's seeing Jack? And here Lena is supposed to be her best friend."

"While the cat's away the mice will play," Jessie offered candidly.

"We tried to talk her out of going to Europe, didn't we?" Jenny stops walking. "What a back stabbing low life bitch!" Jenny was furious.

Jake walks up to them. "What's up?" As he looks at Jenny's face.

"I told her. It seems Tom suspected something of the sort, and broke up with her at the party. He doesn't know who though." Jessie answered truthfully.

"Come on, I want to show you some of the property before it gets dark." He takes her hand as Mike and Dan walk over to them.

"Okay," she smiles at him, and looking at Mike, "how do you like your new job?"

"It's great. I've been waiting for Jake's dad to decide when he was ready to cut back his hours. It's a job I've always wanted.

"Your dad is cutting back?" She looked at Jake.

"We started talking about the job. Remember? And somebody got huffy, and then we ended up side tracked before I could explain why dad hired him." Jake explained patiently.

She was quiet for a moment. "I guess you're right. But why is he retiring?"

"He said it's time he and mother do a little traveling. He turned the shop over to me, and we hired Mike. He's a good mechanic, and a good worker." Jake smacks him on the back. "Besides, this way I can keep my eye on him."

"But what about college?" Shelly asked a little confused.

"I think I'll put that on hold for now. This is really what I want to do. Work with old cars."

"You don't mind?" Shelly asked Jenny.

"Not at all." As she smiled at him. "If this makes him happy. I'm happy. And isn't that what life is about? Doing whatever makes you happy?"

"You're right," Shelly answered.

"Why are you up here?" Mike asked Jake again.

"Well, I was testing the motor in that car," pointing at the Mercury, "when I saw this lane, and drove up to check it out. It looked as if someone was going to build, and didn't. I liked it, and decided I'd try to find out who owned it. I'd like to purchase it." He pulled Jessie close. "And since I intend on marrying Jessie, I brought her here to show it to her."

She smiled into his eyes. "Did you find out who owns it?"

"Not yet," he smiled back. "I wanted you to see it first."

They explored for a while, and finally Jake said, "it's supper time. Do you two want to join us?"

Mike looks at Jenny. "Do you mind?"

"Heck no! I'm hungry too." She laughed.

"Me too," Shelly spoke up.

"What's new? You're always hungry." Jake smarted off at her.

"Ha, ha," Shelly faked a laugh.

"You guys want to ride with us?"

"We'd better not. I don't have my chain with me, and you never can tell when someone might find it up here. Not locked." Patting his bike seat.

"Where are you going?" Jenny asked.

"The steak house. Dan's hungry for a steak." Jessie answered.

"Ummm, you're making my mouth water." Jenny laughs.

"We'll follow you." Mike gets on his bike.

"Let's do it." Jake helps Jessie into the car.

"This car is awesome." Jessie said again.

Jake just smiled as he drove down the lane. "So how much did you tell Jenny?"

"Just that we knew who Lynn was seeing. No particulars, just that we knew." Jessie answered.

"Jenny sure did look furious. I'll bet she has a temper." Jake looks at Jessie.

"She does. And none of us are too pleased with Lynn right now anyway. So this really ticked her off bad."

"Why are none of you too pleased with her?" Dan asked curiously.

"She's always trying to get someone else's boyfriend." Shelly spat. "She's non content until she's seduced someone. And Lena isn't even here to fight her."

"She's back," Jake stated.

"What?" Jessie and Shelly looked at one another. "When did this happen?" Jessie asked.

"We saw her the day before yesterday?" Jake looks at Dan.

"And she never called us. I wonder what's up with that?" Shelly sounded hurt.

"I can't imagine what happened. Nobody said anything at the beach the other day either." Jessie tried to be objective. "Let's ask Jenny. Maybe she'll know something."

As Jake pulls into the restaurant, "here we are. My mouth is watering already."

Jessie pushes on him. "Get out. I'm starving." She laughs.

They enjoyed a good meal for a change. They enjoyed having Mike and Jenny with them, and when they were done eating, the girls went to the powder room.

"Alright. You have to tell me how you found out about Lynn."

Jessie looks at Shelly. Not sure just what she should tell her. Sighing, "Jake was over at Salinas a few days ago, and saw them coming out of a motel six."

"Isn't she just a bitch? I hope one day she finds someone special, and he cheats on her. Actually, I hope he leaves her ass!" Jenny spat vehemently.

"Did you know Lena was home?" Jessie asked her.

"No. Is she?" Jenny said in disbelief.

"Jake says she is. He saw her day before yesterday."

"And she didn't let anyone know? That's odd."

"We thought so too." Shelly agreed.

"You know her rehearsal dinner is coming up in a couple of days. Maybe she's been busy with that." Jenny was making excuses, and they all knew it.

"How can Lynn face her?" Shelly asks as they leave the restroom.

"Very easily, I'm sure." Jenny smirked. "I think it's time to end my friendship with her. Pam and I were talking about it at the party the other night. She's just gotten way out of hand. And it's like she's on this mission to get any and every man she can."

"She won't get mine." Shelly bragged.

"No, and that bugs her to no end."

"Good," Shelly answered simply. "That makes me so happy."

The fellas are waiting on them, and they pay their bills.

As they walk out, Jessie whispers to Jake, "I think we should stop at the house. Don't you?"

"I was going to suggest that. There might be some word by now." He answered quietly. "I'd better take the car back first.'

"Okay. We can't have your dad worrying." She smiled.

"I have to take the car back, and get mine," Jake said to Mike. "What are you doing?"

"We're going for a ride right now. Maybe we can stop by later?"

"Sure," Jake said as he looked as Jessie and winked.

Jessie hugged Jenny. "You guys be careful out there."

"Why don't you guys get bikes so we can ride together?" Mike asked Jake and Dan. "Or don't you like them?"

"Yeah, but I just never thought about it before." Dan shrugs.

"I hope you will now." Jenny said to Jake. "It would be nice to have friends to ride with."

"It's a pretty nice Harley, isn't it?" Dan asked as he walked around and looked it over. "Nice." shaking his head.

"well, we'd better get moving." Jake takes Jessie's arm, and helps her into the car. "See you later, maybe." nodding at Mike.

"Catch you later," Mike said.

Shelly and Jessie wave as they pull away.

The ride to Jake's house was rather, a quiet one. Everybody seemed preoccupied with something, and none wanted to break the silence. Jake pulls into the drive, and opens the garage door. After he parks the car, and locks up, he says, "be right back," as he goes into the house. "Mike seems to be setting down." Shelly looks at Dan. "Is it because he's working with you two?"

"We hope. He's really a good guy. He just hangs with the wrong crowd most of the time."

"I'm glad he's working with you two. It might help him in his relationship with Jenny." Jessie sighed.

"She seems happier, doesn't she?" Shelly asked a statement.

Jake returns, and gets into his car. "Okay. Now to your house."

When they pull up to Jessie's house, there is still no one home. She lets them in, and checks the caller ID. There was several calls from the police department, and a couple from Donna, but nothing else.

"I wonder if they could be at Dave's house? Mother wouldn't call me from over there either. She trusts me, and I told her she's a big girl. So I know that I wouldn't hear from her unless I was really important."

"Call over there and see. This is the time to make an exception to the rule." Jake ordered.

"I don't know his number."

"Look it up," Shelly offered.

"Can't do that either. I don't know his last name." She paused. "Wait a minute. He just sold her insurance, his name will be on there." She gets into the desk, and laying on top, is a copy of her forms. "His name is David Gilbert."

Jake gets the phone book. "Here it is," as he holds the book out to Jessie.

"You know what guys? Why don't we just ride over by there? That way if they are there, we won't disturb them."

"Let me call the police department first." Jake said as he picked up the phone. "Yes, this is Jake Lansing. Is there a chance that the chief is around?" He paused. "No. I'm at Jessica's house right now." He paused again. "She's getting someone to talk to me."

"Jake? This is Sgt. Adson. We don't have anything to tell you yet. We're still looking, but he probably is well away by now. The chief wants you to call him at this number. Got a pen? This is his cell phone, seven five nine - four one zero three. It's not urgent, but he'd like you to call."

"Okay. Thank you, sir." He replaced the phone. "He said there is nothing to report to us, but Mike wants us to call him."

"First, we are going to Dave's to see if they are there." Jessie said in determination. "Or I go alone."

"Jessie!" Jake threatened.

She stood her ground. Grabbing her keys, and heading for the door.

Jake grabbed her, and took her keys from her. "God, Jessie! We're going over there!"

"Then let's do it. I feel something is wrong." She looks at Shelly. "You know that terrible dread I told you about? Well it's right here." She placed her hand over her chest. "So can we please go?"

She didn't even bother to lock the door. She just knows that they must get there. She had a sinking feeling in her heart, and she knew that it meant something was wrong. To make things worse, Dave lived clear across town. Even thought it was about a ten minute drive, Jessie felt like it took forever. Dave lived in a development area on the outskirts of town, and as they turned in, Shelly gave a low whistle.

"Look at this place, would you!"

Jake smiled. "If you want to see some dream homes, here's the place to come to."

"Okay everybody, be alert. We all know what Dave's car looks like so watch for it in case we can't see the numbers." Jessie sounded urgent. They rode back in a ways when she pointed. "There. Down the street. Now drive slowly so we don't miss it."

Jake looks at her. "What do you think you'll find?"

"Nothing I hope." Shaking her head. "But, I can't get the picture of it standing before me, covered in blood, out of my head. I don't want that part to be true, but everything else has been right on."

"Yeah," Shelly whispered. "It has been."

"There it is!" Dan pointed at Dave's car.

"Well at least we know they're home." Jake said as he drove by very slowly. He went up the street and turned around.

"Stop, Jake. Please, just do it." Pleading with him. "I have to look and see that they are okay."

He pulls over, and shuts off the car. She gets out, and slowly walks up to the house, and looking in the dining room window, freezes. She turns, and falls to the ground. Jake and the others are out of the car in an instant. Running to her, he pulls her against him.

"What, honey?" He cradled her.

"Call mike now! He's in there." He's got them, just like I felt."

Dan and Shelly peer in the window. "My God!" Dan exclaimed.

Dave is lying on the floor. He is covered with blood. From all appearances, he seems dead. Carol is sitting in a chair, her hands and feet are taped. The woman pacing back and forth in front of her has on that pink polka dot, and blonde wig. She has blood on her face, the dress, and she has a knife. In her left hand. She seems to be very agitated.

Carol tried to speak to her, but Alice is slobbering all over her, as she puts her finger to her mouth, and shakes her head.

"Shhh, don't speak." Then she laughs again, as she stands sneering. "Wouldn't matter what you said anyhow. I've got you right where I want you, and soon," getting right in her face again, "that'll be dead." She points to Dave. "Just like him!" She stood, looking at Carol for a long, long moment. "You still don't recognize me do you?" As she straightened up, and paced again.

Carol shakes her head, studying Alice's face. "No," she whispered.

"Well, look good now!" Alice sneers as she rips the wig off.

Carols eyes widen, "Allen!" She whispered. "But thou…" She didn't finish the sentence.

"You though wrong. All of you." He sneers in her face. "I got out. On good behavior at that." He laughs evilly. "Imagine that. On good behavior." He's still laughing as he walks over to Dave, and kicks him. "Bastard!" He hissed at him. "Even he didn't like me!"

"What happened to the other girls?" Carol asked apprehensively.

"They got theirs, believe me!" Shaking his head up and down. "They got exactly what they deserved!" He wheeled on her again. "And now it's your turn." He hissed in her face. There was drool dripping from his mouth. "Maybe I should kiss you now. While you can't push me away. Or maybe, I should do something else." He looks down at her breast. He placed his hand just below her chin, and moves it down slowly.

Carol tried to move away, but he pinned her to the back of the chair. He puts the knife to her throat.

"Still appalled by me?" He hissed at her.

Carol swallows. "I was never appalled by you, Allen. I just didn't like you. There's a difference."

He jerked his hand back and turned away. "Maybe your pretty little girl will like me. She quite luscious, you know." He sneers at her. "Just like you were back then." Turning to look at her. "Yes, maybe I'll do that. Call her to come over here."

"Don't touch her!" Carol said through clenched teeth.

"Maybe I have been dreaming of her. With her cute little figure. She's a dream." He starts singing. "Row, row, row your boat, gently down the stream. Marilee, merrily, merrily, merrily, life is but a dream." He stops and looks at her again. "I bet you wish this was a dream, don't you, Carol?" Putting the knife against her cheek, and pressing it in. Blood trickled out. "You can stop dreams, but you can't stop this. Can you, Carol?" He started dancing in circles. "What do you say to that?"

"Why are you doing this?" She asked calmly. She thought maybe if she tried a different approach, he would be more inclined to listen. "I was never mean to you. I asked you, please, not to call me. I begged you not to follow me. I had a boyfriend, whom I married. And never, in any way, did I leave you to believe that I liked you, or wanted to be with you." She sighs deeply. "Besides, you never knew which one us you wanted. Me, or Jamie, or Anne." "That's not true!" He spat at her. "I only did that to be near you!" Pushing the knife into her cheek again. "But no! You all thought yourselves to good for me. Well, Miss Carol. I showed them. You bet I did!"

"You are truly mad." Carol exclaimed.

He pulled back. "Is that what I am? Well, fancy that. I'm mad!"

He's laughing uncontrollably as he paces back and forth in front of her. "And one more thing. That accident your husband had?"

Shaking his head back and forth. "No, no, no!" His voice reaching a high pitch.

"Oh, Allen, you didn't?" The tears started flowing down her cheeks, and mixing with the blood, and streaking.

"Oh, Carol, I did," as he wiped the tears, looking quite smug.

"You are as insane as they say you are. How could you do this?" She wept silently.

"You know what else?" He grins from ear to ear. "Oh, I do think you are going to like this one." He starts laughing hysterically. "They didn't release me at all. No, never! I did it myself! All by myself. I took her dress and wig." He picks up the wig, and holds it out to her. He lifts the corner of the dress. "See? These were hers. And I just walked," he motions with his fingers, "right out of there." He starts laughing so hard, he falls to his knees. Spit was running down his chin.

Carol is sobbing silently, and has her head lowered, so she doesn't see him leave the room. Noticing the quiet, she looks up. He's gone. She hears Dave moan, and looks at him. He opens his eyes, and tries to move.

"Stay down," she whispers. "He thinks you're dead." She catches a movement at the window. "Thank God they are here." Dave looks at her. She motions to the window with her head. He raises up and looks over. With a sigh of relief, he lays back.

The police have the house surrounded. When mike sees him leave the room, "Now! Go! Go! Go!" And they bust into the house at the same time. Front and back. Mike runs to Carol and Dave.

"I'm alive," Dave said weakly, as he rolls over, and looks at Carol. "Are you okay?"

Mike takes the tape off of her, and she kneels by Dave, and takes his head into her lap, "Yes, I'm okay. And you just lay there and be quiet. I couldn't bear it if I lost you too." Tears are streaming down her face. He smiles at her as he closes his eyes.

Sgt. Adson is pushing Allen ahead oh him as they come into the room. "We finally got him. After all this time, we finally got him!"

The EMT's came in with a stretcher, and Jessie runs for her mother, and hugs her tight.

"Oh, mother, I thought I had lost you!" She squeezed her so hard, that her mother took ahold of her arms.

Hey, hey! You're crushing me!" Carol laughs at her.

Jessie pulls back. "Is Dave going to be alright?"

One of the EMT's looks at her. "It's hard to tell yet. He's lost a lot of blood, and we don't know the extent of his injuries."

"He'll be fine." Carol pats her hand reassuringly.

Mike helps her from the house, as they put wrist and ankle cuffs on Allen, and lead him to the cruiser.

"He's not going anywhere, and you can bet he'll never get a chance to hurt anyone else again." Mike stared hard at him.

The cart with Dave is stopped by Carol. Placing her lips to his cheeks, she whispers, "I'll be down as soon as I get cleaned up."

"Do you need to go to the hospital?" Mike asked Carol as the cruiser pulled away.

"No. I'll go home and clean up, and then go to the hospital for Dave." She looked sadly at Jessie. "Besides, I have to talk with Jessica about something, and I'd like to get it done and over with."

"I'll need your statement. I can wait until tomorrow if you'd like." Mike volunteered.

"Thank you. That would be best." Carol smiled wanly.

Jake helps them into the car. The ride home was filled with a heavy silence. All faces, solemn and sad.

As they enter the house, Carol looks at Jessie. "Before I get cleaned up, come into the living room and sit down."

Jessie felt a dread creep over her again, and felt her nerves start to jump. "What is it, mother?"

She took a deep sigh, and said, I learned tonight... That your father's accident was no accident at all."

"What do you mean?" As she turns paler.

"Allen told me that he killed him." She said sadly. "And he knew it would rip my heart out when he did. Laughing about it."

"That bastard!" Jake said vehemently.

"Oh, mother." Jessie wailed as she went into her arms. "We knew something wasn't right. Didn't we?"

"Yes, sweetie, we knew." Kissing her head. "And now that we know, we can really start to heal." "Why did he want to hurt you so badly?" Jessie asked through a sob.

"It's a long story from my school days." Standing. "I really should get cleaned up and go to Dave. I'll tell you everything tomorrow. Okay?"

Jessie shakes her head and sadly watches her mother leave the room. Her eyes come back to Jake, who takes her in his arms, and gently cradles her. Running his fingers through her hair, and kissing the top of her head.

She sighs. "It's over." Raising her eyes to his. "It's finally over. The dreams should be gone now. They should be gone." Sighing sadly, she lays her head on his shoulder.

"Yes they should be." Kissing her again. "And I hope you never have occasion to dream again."

"I think we all feel that emotion." Dan said meaningly.

"Are we going to the hospital with mother?" Jessie asked.

"We should. Don't you think?" Jake asked in reply.

Carol came down the steps. "Well, I'm leaving now."

Jessie gets up. "We're coming too, mother." She touches her face. "do these hurt much?"

"No. They burnt at first," placing her hand gently on them, "but now they're alright. Thank God they weren't any deeper. I might have scares."

Jessie hugs her. "I'm so glad you're alright, mother."

"Me too, sweetie. Now let's get down there. Okay?"

"And I'm so glad you found someone else to love." Taking her hand as they walk out. "He seems so right for you."

Smiling, she hugs Jessie. "I think so too."

Jake puts his arms around both women as they leave the house. Feeling very much the protector right now. Wanting nothing else to happen to these two beautiful ladies.

"Hi," Carol smiles at him as they enter the room. "How are you feeling?"

"As well as can be expected I guess." He winced.

"You didn't fair so well, huh?" Jessie smiled wanly.

"No. Afraid not. What hurts is where he kicked me in the ribs."

"Your stab wounds don't hurry?" Jessie frowned.

"The one here does a little." Pointing at what was a gap in his left arm. "I thank the good Lord he didn't aim so good or it just might have been in my heart."

"Why such fury on you I wonder?" Jake asked, puzzled.

"I'm sure it was because of Carol." He winced as a pain hit him in the side.

Do you want me to call a nurse?" Carol asks concerned.

Dave shook his head.. "No. They're going to be taking me to x-ray to see if my ribs are broken. I hope it's soon." He had no sooner said that than they came into the room.

"Okay, Mr. Gilbert, we're ready for you in x-ray." The nurse looked at Carol. "You can wait in the waiting room down the hall, and we'll let you know, as soon as we can, when to come back."

"It wouldn't surprise me a bit if they're broken. She kicked, I mean he kicked him several times." Carol, looking angry. "When I think of what he has done to the lives of so many people." She sighs. "It just makes me extremely angry."

One of the nurses steps up to her, and looks at the cuts on her face. "have you had the doctor look at these?"

"No. I went home and washed them out." Carol answered.

"Let me see if he would take a quick look."

"Okay." Carol looked at Jessie, and raised her shoulders.

"It's probably for the best, mother. You might need a shot or something. You know, in case the knife was dirty."

"I didn't think about that."

"Can't be too careful these days." Dan offered.

"That's for sure." Jessie agreed.

The nurse came back, followed by the doctor. He took Carol's face in his hands, and turned it back and forth, and gently touched the cuts.

"I think we should give her an antibiotic cream, and a tetanus shot. The cream will keep it from getting infected. That will also keep it from scarring. Put it on three times a day, and rub it in. You'll be fine."

"Thank you." Carol smiled. She made a face at Jessie. "A shot. I hate shots." She whispered.

"Who doesn't?" Jessie laughed. "We'll go ahead out to the waiting room. Come out as soon as you're done."

Jake takes her hand as they walk down the hall. Shelly and Dan close behind.

"Poor Dave," Shelly sympathizes. "He seemed in so much pain."

"I know. I hope that's all that is wrong with him. If he was kicked hard enough to break ribs, there could be other damage." Jessie offered.

"I hope not." Shelly shuddered. "Hey, let's get something to drink. You know he'll be a while, probably your mother too, so we might as well relax."

"I could use something to drink. All the excitement made me thirsty." Dan answered. Shaking his head. "I still can't believe that guy. How could you have such rage in you like that. And over what?"

"What is puzzling is why he waited so many years to do what he did. Mother is forty-one. She graduated when she was eighteen. That was twenty-three years ago." Jessie was clearly puzzled.

"Maybe he just never had the opportunity to break out before this. Maybe when Alice Watson showed up that day, in that dress, it triggered something in him. A memory of your mother wearing something similar, maybe." Dan pondered.

Jessie shuddered. "I hate to think what was on his mind. But twenty-three years is a long time to harbor a grudge."

"You can say that again." Jake emphasized.

"Ah, here's the snack room." Dan said pointing at it.

"Your mother will find us, won't she, Jess?" Shelly asked as they sat down.

"I'm sure she will."

"So. Now, what will we do for excitement, Jessie?" Jake smiles at her. "Since you've given us a taste of it, I like it."

"Me too." Shelly said willingly. "Too much so, I'm afraid."

"Yeah. What will we do? Hmmm. Well we'll definitely have to think of something. But no more dreams!" She emphasized. "No more dreams!"

"I didn't like that part either." Shelly said, shaking her head.

Jessie locked eyes with her. "You saw first hand, didn't you?"

"Did I ever!" Shelly laughs.

"Sorry," Jessie apologized.

"I'm glad I was there."

"When did that happen?" Jake asked. Looking from one to another.

"The other night, when I stayed over. Not meaning to be ignorant or anything, but I'm glad it was you, not me." Shelly stated.

"I think it was a good thing it wasn't you. Your will is not quite as strong as mine." Jessie said matter of factly.

"I know." Shelly smiled sheepishly.

"I hate shots." Carol said as she walked into the room. "I figured I'd find you here." As she gets a drink, and sits down. "Ouch." She winced.

"Got it in the butt, huh?" Jessie said laughing.

"It's not funny. And yes," as she reaches back, "in the butt."

The others laugh at her.

"You're so funny, mother." Jessie laughs.

"Glad you think so." Carol smirked back.

"How's your face feeling?" Shelly asked concerned.

"It burns a bit. They put some cream on it to help out, 'til I can get my prescription filled."

"Do you think, maybe, we should get back to the waiting room in case they come for us?" Jessie asked.

"That might be a good idea." Carol stood up.

"I suppose they'll keep Dave overnight, huh, mother?"

"I would imagine so. If for nothing else, but observation. The pounding he took was pretty bad."

"How did he get into such a position, mother? I mean, Dave's a big man." Jessie was clearly puzzled.

"Allen hit him from behind. Grabbed him around the throat, and put him to him knees. Stabbed him, and kicked at him repeatedly. I tried to help, and he sent me flying." Tears welled in her eyes. "I could do nothing."

"Hey, you tried." Jake reached for her hand. "That's all that could be expected under the circumstanced."

"Yes, mother. So don't you go blaming yourself for any of this. Do you hear me?" Jessie said firmly.

Her mother laughed then. "Yes, daughter, I hear you."

The nurse walked up and said, "you can come back now."

They were on their feet in seconds, and headed for Dave's room.

"Hi," Carol smiled at him.

"Hi," he smiled back. "They're keeping me overnight."

"I figured they would," as she takes his hand.

"He has two broken ribs, and two deep wounds. But the bump on the back of his head is why we're keeping him. Just for observation."

"So you might as well go home, and I'll call you in the morning when I get released." He closed his eyes.

Carol leaned over, and kissed his forehead. "You're probably tired anyhow."

"Well, they gave me a shot, and I'm starting to feel it." Smiling wanly at her.

Smiling into his eyes, "I love you," Carol whispered.

"I love you too. Now go home. I'll be fine." he pulls her head down, and kisses her. "Good night."

"Night." As she turns from the bed.

"Night, Dave," the others wave as they leave the room.

"I think we'll wait 'til tomorrow to have that talk kids, I'm tired, and think I'd like to go to bed myself."

"Sure, mother. We can wait. We might be biting nails, but we'll wait." Jessie laughs.

"What choice do we have?" Jake asks jokingly.

"None what's so ever." Carol laughs back.

"Well then. I guess we'll see you in the morning." Jake said.

"Night, kids." Carol smiled at them.

"Night." They answered.

"I'm thinking we should go too, Dan. It's late, and none of us has had much sleep the last couple of days."

"Me too," Shelly said. "I'm exhausted after all that's happened."

"What do you think, Jessie? Are you ready to turn in?" Jake rocks her back and forth.

"Yeah. I guess so. But come over early, and we'll go have breakfast, and hear the whole story about this Allen character."

"Alright." He kissed her lightly, and pulled her to the door. "See you in the morning then."

She kissed him goodnight. "Night everybody." She waved as they left her drive way.

Jessie mounted the steps slowly, thinking about Dave, and prayed that he would have a comfortable night. She knew that she was also looking forward to bed. If for no other reason than to see if she dreamed any tonight. She undressed, and touching Jake's picture, laid down, and looking to heaven whispered, "Good night, Jesus. I love you." And she closed her eyes.

****